DOCTOR WHO

THE GIGGLE

THE GIGGLE

Based on the BBC television adventure
The Giggle by Russell T Davies

JAMES GOSS

BBC
BOOKS

BBC Books, an imprint of Ebury Publishing
20 Vauxhall Bridge Road
London SW1V 2SA

BBC Books is part of the Penguin Random House group of companies whose
addresses can be found at global.penguinrandomhouse.com

Penguin
Random House
UK

To the Losers

Doctor Who is produced in Wales by Bad Wolf
with BBC Studios Productions.

Executive Producers: Russell T Davies, Julie Gardner,
Jane Tranter, Phil Collinson & Joel Collins

First published by BBC Books in 2023

www.penguin.co.uk

A CIP catalogue record for this book is available from the British Library
ISBN 9781785948473

Editorial Director: Albert DePetrillo
Project Editor: Steve Cole
Cover Design: Two Associates
Cover illustration: Anthony Dry

Typeset by Rocket Editorial Ltd

Printed and bound in Great Britain by Clays Ltd, Elcograf S.p.A.
The authorised representative in the EEA is Penguin Random House Ireland,
Morrison Chambers, 32 Nassau Street, Dublin D02 YH68

MIX
Paper | Supporting
responsible forestry
FSC® C018179
www.fsc.org

Penguin Random House is committed to a sustainable future
for our business, our readers and our planet. This book is made
from Forest Stewardship Council® certified paper.

Move 1

This is the end.

Is that cheating?

Well, it depends on how you play the game. How many moves ahead can you see?

For Charles Bannerjee, the end is a street in London, 1925. If he hadn't been hurrying, if it hadn't been raining so hard, if he hadn't forgotten his umbrella, if he hadn't soaked his shoe when he stepped into the gutter to avoid a muttering old lady; if all these little things hadn't happened, then he'd have gone to the department store on Regent Street. Wider choice, better prices. Slightly further walk.

But no. He saw the toyshop just in front of him (why had he never noticed it before?) and he changed his plans. MR EMPORIUM'S TOYSHOP was a candy-striped beacon against the drab wet stone, its golden windows crowded with all the magic of childhood beckoning him in – waving dolls and smiling teddy bears, little tin horses dangling from a toy carousel and a little red motor car spinning on a silver thread.

Charles pushed against the door and felt a little thrill as the bell went ting-a-ling. Last time he'd been in a place like this, his mother had been leading him by the hand to give him a little consolation prize on the last day of the holidays. He was surprised that the toyshop still towered over and wrapped itself around him, as though he were stepping into the jaws of a funfair monster, all red-and-white stripes and crammed mahogany shelves. Normally, revisiting childhood spots, he found them smaller, tireder, somehow sadder. But this toyshop was bursting with awe and wonder and—

Poot poot!

A little toy train raced around the ceiling – the exact colour – no, the exact train he'd received for his twelfth birthday. A brightly boxed jigsaw of Brighton beach, so vivid he felt if he squinted he'd see his toddler self with a bucket and spade. A pinboard horse derby, all the little horses in mid-leap; two horses were leaping a cardboard fence carrying a little toy hearse behind them, and there was even a little balsa wood coffin inside – the exact same sort as his father had been buried in. And was that a tiny tin nameplate? If he leaned forward and squinted he could maybe read the name …

DING!

Someone thumped the bell on the counter. A figure sprang up from behind the desk – a living jack-in-the-box. This could only be Mr Emporium – a handsome, kindly man beaming with joy and twinkling from his shiny pince-nez glasses to his brightly polished leather apron. Even his bow tie sparkled like a Christmas bauble.

Mr Emporium was laughing. Laughing at the world. Laughing at Charles. 'Ah! Guten tag, guten tag, komm into dee warm!' The affected German accent was sticky as mulled wine. 'It is ge-raining is it not? All of de water all splishy splashy! Tsk!' A tiny tut, as Charles dripped rain onto the ancient oak floorboards. 'Now, vot can I helpensie mit? Beholt!' A sweep took in the entirety of the shop, and Charles stepped back. The man was filling the store, and Charles felt like a lost child, with a hot hand full of farthings and a stammering urge to ask if they were enough for a ball. 'Ve haff everysing! Everysing you could be ge-wanten. Ve haff dolls! Zuch beautifool pink-faced dollen, ja?'

A beautifully manicured hand extended from a crisp shirt cuff and pointed – *ein, zwei, drei* – at three shelves crammed with dolls, their glass eyes sparkling. Charles wondered if he should wave back at them.

'We haff dee compendium of game! Mit dee dice and de snakesn un ladderz and dee rules…' He snatched up a box and rattled it, the painted snakes on the cover dancing. 'Dee rules, zey are fery fery importanten, de rules, don't you sink? Also!' The box was thrown aside as Mr Emporium picked up a morose teddy bear and a toy horse's head on a cantering stick. 'Ve haffen de teddy bears und dee hobby-horsen. Who does not vant a hobby-horsen to go clippety-clop down the strasse, ja?'

He rode the horse back and forth behind the counter.

Charles felt, all of a sudden, a little dizzy; the man's

3

show was all too much, like brandy sauce on plum pudding. He'd come for one thing and one thing alone, and he didn't need the full song and dance. He'd not come to buy a toy but a prop – he needed something that looked vaguely human and now he saw it, set apart from the little princess dolls: Stooky Bill. A ventriloquist's dummy, two feet high, with a pinstripe suit and a papier mâché smile, little puppet family gathered around him, dusty but – yes, the old boy would be perfect for what he needed. He plucked him from the shelf and took him to the counter.

'I just want this, really,' said Charles, feeling a little apologetic.

'Ah!' Mr Emporium gleamed. 'Stooky Bill, meine favoriten! But –' and the saddest frown – 'vill you leave dee family all alone? Poor Stooky Sue! And dee poor liddle Stooky Babbies, you vill leave dem vizout Papa? Dee vidow und orphans will be ge-crying!' Mr Emporium gestured to the abandoned dolls and then screwed his hands into his eyes, a pantomime of grief.

'Um, no, just him, thanks.' Charles looked around. Was there anyone else in the shop? Surely there must be some children somewhere – this showmanship couldn't be just for him.

'Du bist cruel!' Mr Emporium wagged a finger at Charles. 'I liken you.'

Shaking his head at the grief of the world, the toymaker began wrapping Stooky Bill in brown paper and string. Charles noticed something. Something odd and curiously repellent.

'Is that real hair?'

'Ja ja, I vox ge-sticking on dee hair meinself.' Mr Emporium ran his fingers through the doll's locks. 'I cut it from dee head of a beautiful lady. She vill not miss it,' he sniggered. 'But den, she vill never miss anythink ever again!'

He carried on giggling, trying to cover his mouth with his hands, but the giggles wouldn't be stifled.

Charles pressed on politely. 'And how much is the dummy?'

'Sixpence.' Mr Emporium dropped his hand, and the smile vanished. 'But I really must apologise for the rain outside.' A long pause between them. 'You must be used to sunnier climes.'

'I was born in Cheltenham,' Charles said with dignity. He was used to this. His parents had left Kerala's tropical storms for Gloucestershire's stately drizzle. England had offered them a polite but chilly welcome. Once his schoolfellows had realised he wasn't the offspring of a Maharajah, he'd stopped being exciting and become a plaything to torment. The visits to the toyshop on the final day of the holidays had been the last bit of comfort before eight weeks of well-bred cruelty.

Here we were again.

'Oh!' Mr Emporium beamed. 'By the looks of it, it's very sunny there too.'

'Your accent seems to have slipped,' Charles pointed out, handing over the money. 'I think we've said enough. I'll just take him and go, thank you.'

He snatched up his parcel and headed for the door.

Mr Emporium's voice, cod-German again, reached him as he tugged at the door. 'I hope dee kiddies enchoy him!'

'It's not for children.' Charles allowed himself a bit of grandeur. 'It's for my employer. He lives around the corner. You might have heard of him? Mr John Logie Baird.'

'Ooooooo!' Mr Emporium was impressed, all too impressed. 'Dee Inventor-man! Wunderbar! Vot is he being inventing now?'

'Well...' Charles figured there was no harm in telling the man. 'It's complicated. It's this new thing called... Tele-Vision.'

'Vell!' Mr Emporium was bursting with smiles. 'Vot a game ve are playink. Vot a vonderful, vonderful game!'

He started giggling again. As Charles headed out into the rain, the giggles followed him.

'Poor wee Stooky Bill.'

Inside the world's first television studio, a genial Scot named John Logie Baird was dismembering the ventriloquist's dummy with huge excitement. Although his invention of balloon shoes and the glass razorblade hadn't taken off, the Tele-Vision was about to catch fire.

'Stooky's a Scottish word,' he said, tearing the head off and setting it on a pole. 'D'you know what Stooky means?'

Charles Bannerjee, dutifully writing everything down on a clipboard, listened patiently. Baird liked to talk while he set things up, distracting himself from worries about what would happen – what if the bulbs over the puppet overheated and exploded (again)? What if the spinning disc that captured the image fell off? What if they fused the entire building's wiring?

'The word comes from Stucco. As in, plaster. But it's come to mean stupid and slow, like Billy boy's an idiot.' John stood back, his wild eyes barely kept in his skull, admiring the head on a pole like a cartoon cannibal's trophy. Then he and Charles retreated, following the tangled mess of cable through the attic flat to a tiny bedroom where, on top of a sideboard, sat the world's first Tele-Vision.

Currently there were no channels and nothing was on.

They settled down in front of it to wait.

'But our Stooky Bill can't be that daft,' John said, with the ghost of a grin. 'He's about to make history. Ready?'

Charles nodded, and John took a deep, even breath. 'As my old dad would say, may God go with us.' He turned on the power, and Tele-Vision began.

In the living room, the big bank of lights glowed fiercely. The disc began to spin. Underneath the blaze of lights, Stooky Bill's head stared ahead, calm.

In the bedroom, the face of Stooky Bill appeared on

7

the Tele-Vision monitor, bobbing up like a corpse in a pond.

'I did it,' John breathed out. 'I did it.'

Charles always worried. Even from this distance he could feel the heat coming from the living room lamps. 'We're not going to catch fire, are we?'

'That's why we need Stooky Bill,' John reassured him. 'All those lights. No man could sit underneath that temperature.'

The air began to fill with the smell, first of hot dust, and then of something worse – of burning hair.

Underneath the blazing lamps, the glue of the puppet began to melt like caramel, the varnish blistering, the paint bubbling. But, fundamentally, the image of Stooky Bill on the screen remained the same.

John leaned in, frowning. 'If I'm to prove that television works, I'll need a moving image.'

The head of Stooky Bill jerked forward towards them.

The two men took a jump back, then gasped in relief – the glue holding the jaw together had fallen away, leaving the puppet's mouth hanging open.

'Gave me quite a shock.' John wiped his forehead. 'Imagine. If he could talk. That wee chap's about to change the world. Imagine what he would say.'

On screen, Stooky Bill stared out silently. Maybe gaping. Maybe screaming.

Maybe laughing.

Move 2

Go back two spaces to London in the here and now.

A very puzzled man is standing outside a time machine which is also a blue police box, watching the world end. The man is called the Doctor, and he has had what his best friend would call *A Day*.

Yesterday, the Doctor had been a woman standing on an exploding asteroid saving the universe, as a result of which she'd changed bodies. This happened to the Doctor from time to time, usually when stuff got in the way such as a death ray or rapidly approaching ground. The thing is, the new body was normally a new one.

The body the Doctor was currently wearing wasn't new so much as vintage. Upcycled. It was the second time the process of physical regeneration had left him with this body, which was surprising and unusual and needed a bit of getting used to.

Instead, there'd been the Daleks and then, just when he'd thought he might catch a breath, he'd bumped into his best friend. She hadn't seen him for fifteen years.

The last time he'd seen Donna Noble had also been the last time he'd worn this body. He'd had to lock away all her memories of him inside her mind, as that mind had bitten off more than it could chew. And, if there was one thing that Donna Noble really loved, it was chewing over things.

Anyway, he'd regained both this body and his best friend. He'd safely unlocked Donna's memories of him, and they'd saved the world from the Meep, and been on a trip to the edge of the universe, which should have taken them minutes – only, when they stepped out of the TARDIS, the world had gone mad.

Which was why the Doctor was standing outside his time machine having A Day. His handsome face haggard, his eyes wary, his hair ready to run for the hills.

Donna laid one hand on his arm. She'd had A Day too: she'd started off worrying about work, her daughter and her mother's cooking, and now here she was, having fought off two alien races and been impersonated by a bizarre entity. She had sort of missed this, sort of not.

She had the Doctor back in her life and it was brilliant, it was mad; but also, it worried her. There was something about him. He seemed more skinny than ever, as if his soul hung off his bones. She sensed there was something he wasn't telling her. We all have secrets, but the Doctor was a bundle of paper-thin flesh wrapped around them. They'd met *something* at the edge of existence, and after he'd warded it off with an ancient ritual, he hadn't seemed like his old self. His old self would have been thrilled, but this Doctor was nervy. When Donna had given birth to Rose, she'd been like that, living her life from one *What Now?* to the next.

Wilfred Mott had been waiting for them when they'd got back to Camden Market. Donna's best grandfather. (The Doctor knew a thing or two about grandfathers, having been one himself.) An old soldier, Wilf was still holding himself smartly to attention, even in a wheelchair, waiting for the TARDIS (the name for the battered blue time police machine box thing) to finally get back from the thin end of the universe. He'd thrown a smart salute as the box had arrived. A good piece to have on the board.

He was almost crying with relief to see them. 'Oh my goodness! Donna!'

'Gramps!' Donna had told the Doctor that Wilf would be waiting for them whenever they got back. That was the thing about the TARDIS. It had a drag queen's sense of timekeeping, always making a big entrance, just a bit late. And here Donna was, face to face with the loveliest man in the world, and now she could remember all they'd been through together. It was so good to see him, but her grandad looked strained. How long had he been waiting? He'd not missed *Strictly*, had he? No. It was something far worse than that.

The Doctor was equally thrilled to see her grandad. 'Wilfred Mott! Aw, *now* I feel better! Now, nothing is wrong, nothing in the whole wide world. Hello, my old soldier!'

'I never thought I'd see you again.' Wilf was almost crying with happiness. 'After all these years. Oh, Doctor, that lovely face. Like springtime!'

11

The Doctor beamed, but Donna – oh, she could taste it. Something was wrong.

'I knew it. I never lost faith.' Wilf was almost babbling. 'I said, he won't let us down! He'll come back and save us!'

Oh, there it was.

'Save us from what?' the Doctor asked.

In a minute, Donna thought. *First things first.* 'Where's the family? Where's Rose? Are they all right?'

'They're fine, they're safe.' Wilf laid a paw on her hand, and she realised he was shaking. 'I told them to bunker down. I'll keep watch, I said, you save yourselves.'

'Why?' The Doctor looked around, alert, cueing up the apocalypse. 'Is there something wrong?'

At the edge of Donna's vision a group of people had been standing round a coffee van. They'd been shouting their orders, all of them fiddly. Hold this, extra that, the usual, just a bit louder. Only – suddenly – the entire coffee van exploded. Shooting up in the air, cups and cupcakes born aloft on a brown geyser.

She'd just been about to run towards them, when a fireball shot out of the backdoor of a restaurant – chefs and waiters tumbling out, fighting and roaring in the flame.

It was like everyone in the world was taking a turn for the worse at the same time.

Over there, a tour guide was laying about his group with an umbrella, and two women were fighting on the cobbles over a knitted poncho, one sinking her teeth into the other's ear.

'What is it? What's happening?' Donna cried.

Wilf looked up at her, and she saw the sadness and the terror in his kind old eyes. 'It's everything! It's everyone! They're all going mad!' He gripped the Doctor's hand. 'You've got to do something, Doctor! The whole world is coming to an end!'

The Doctor was trying to take everything in, his face guppying like a fish drowning in air. Holding it together with a deep breath, like Donna about to go into the supermarket for the Big Christmas Shop. What was up with him?

There was a roar above them. What now – dinosaurs? Donna looked up. Not again – not another spaceship. No. It was a jet aircraft, impossibly low. It shouldn't be that low. It looked as though it was coming in to land. On Chalk Farm. But that was impossible – surely it'd pull up at the last minute—

The plane landed, smacking into three housing estates, the heat of the fireball washing down towards them.

Oh no, oh god, oh no.

But the people around them didn't even look up from their fights, they just carried on screaming and pummelling at each other.

Donna chewed the air, angry at the entire human race. What the hell was going on?

The Doctor realised the world had gone mad laughing.

A minute ago all had seemed fairly normal, but now he

saw why Wilf had looked so afraid. People were running across the streets, some of them holding shopping trolleys, some of them dragging wheelie luggage, some just rolling together fighting in the streets. Debris was falling from the sky – houses were burning. And everywhere was the sound of sirens.

The Doctor looked away from Wilf to a kindly old lady standing outside a shop – she caught his eye, smiled, and threw a brick through the window. A man stood in the middle of the street, waving a traffic cone around his head and laughing as traffic swerved around him.

Normally Donna Noble was the angriest person in any situation, but right now she was an oasis of calm. Someone had to be in charge.

'What's going on?'

'It all changed, two days ago,' Wilf shook his head. 'Everyone in the world started thinking they were right. All the time! And they won't change their minds. If you try to argue, they go mad.' The old man tightened his grip on the Doctor's hand, imploring. 'You've got to do something.'

Well, first things first. 'We're getting you out of here, Gramps,' Donna said, seizing Wilf's wheelchair and pushing it. A car whizzed past them, not even swerving. It smacked into another car, bumping it out of the way and ploughing through a pavement café before reversing back the way it had come. The Doctor grabbed at the car window.

'Excuse me,' he said to the red-faced driver. 'What are you doing?'

'I can't drive,' the man announced proudly, grinding the gears.

He started to drag the Doctor back into the road. The Doctor kept pace with the car, his voice steady. 'Okay. So. Which means?'

'Well…' The red-faced man got a little redder. 'I pay my taxes, which means I've paid for this road. It is mine. And I will do what I like with it.' The man sped up and dragged the Doctor with him as he weaved across the pavement, the Doctor's legs splaying out as he tried to keep up.

'You'll get yourself killed,' the Doctor protested, clinging limpet-like to the side of the car. He missed cars with running boards. Running boards were nice.

'It's my life, not yours,' the driver snarled, hunching over the steering wheel. 'I'm right, you're wrong, I've always been right.' His face twisted into an ugly smile as he gunned the accelerator, and the car roared jerkily away.

The Doctor was thrown clear and lost his balance. He rolled over and over, between cyclists and a lost dog. He picked himself up and looked around at the mêlée. The motorist had crashed into a cash machine. On a bench a vicar sat, crying and shouting. Old men were kicking each other's walking frames. While their toddlers watched in bemusement, mothers wrestled in the road. A police car pulled up, two sergeants leapt out and started yelling

15

contradictory instructions through their loudhailers, then, when they realised they were at odds, began shouting at each other.

The Doctor tried to gather his thoughts, but they were rolling across the pavement like spilled marbles. In the distance, he saw Donna and Wilf and started to wave. Then he froze. The whole thing, the whole magnificent chaos, if you took one step back and to the side, looked orchestrated. Almost like a dance. A set of moves.

La la la la, la la la la la.

There was something the Doctor could see but couldn't quite see. Two cars sliced past each other, honking angrily, and there, like a grand reveal, stood a figure in top hat and tails, his hands resting on a gold-topped cane. A flash of teeth. Suave and impossibly handsome. The man danced from side to side, then spun around to rest on the cane, smiling in the Doctor's direction.

'Excusez moi, monsieur, oh, je suis terrible. But per'aps you will dance avec moi, ooh-la-la!'

The Doctor stared at the figure. 'Yeah, sorry, no thanks.'

There was too much going on. So many pieces on the board.

The figure did a neat little soft shoe shuffle, and doffed his top hat, rolling it down its arm and following with an elaborate bow. 'Ze game has begun, monsieur, ze formidable game!'

The Doctor moved on. One more madman in among so many madmen. But this one pulled at his thoughts.

Why? What was he missing in all this mess? Where were Wilf and Donna? He'd last seen them a car crash ago.

La la la

The Doctor glanced down. His foot was tapping. He looked out at the sea of surging madness and again, just for a moment, the screaming, the running, the chaos almost formed into a pattern. What was it – yes, that was it –

The sound, the sound he could almost hear, was blotted out by the blades of a helicopter, pressing down on him, the draught rocking him from side to side.

Moments later, it felt like the entire army converged on him, jeeps and trucks pushing through the crowds, soldiers leaping out, running towards him, guns raised.

Now what? thought the Doctor. *Does it ever stop?* How was he going to get out of this?

The soldiers formed a ring around him, guns up, protecting him.

What?

A colonel marched through the chaos, oblivious, barely noticing the screaming old lady he gently pushed to one side. He was a tall, happy giant in a world gone mad.

'Doctor?' he said. 'I'm Colonel Ibrahim of UNIT Squad Five. If you could come this way?'

UNIT! The Unified Intelligence Taskforce. Several bodies ago the Doctor had worked for them, helping them defend the Earth from alien attack. They'd survived changes of government, Cyber-conversion and budget

17

cuts, and here they were, fighting the good fight, in as much as any fight was good.

Normally the Doctor was wary of men with guns. But seeing all this order among the sea of chaos was reassuring. His brain focused. He glimpsed Donna berating some soldiers as Wilf was lifted with care into a truck. 'Never mind me, look after him!'

The music in the corner of his ear faded away.

Only, in that one moment of stillness:

In the crowd, smirking, that dashing man in top hat and tails was waving with a flourish.

And then he was gone. And the noise of the world resumed.

Move 3

A helicopter soared high above London. The Doctor sat in it, still frowning. Donna's concern for him was drawn away by the city below – the fires burning, the screams of madness and anger drifting up to them. Another helicopter flew behind them, the TARDIS dangling from it like a plug on the end of a chain. It didn't look any odder than anything else she'd seen in the last few minutes.

London burned. Flames poked out of windows. People stood on roofs, howling. Cars smashed into each other over and over. Double-decker buses lay toppled in the streets, people thronged the bridges, sometimes diving off, sometimes falling off, sometimes pushed off. She watched two boats down there in the Thames, playing a slow and stupid game of chicken. Neither boat blinked.

The helicopter flew on. Someone had set fire to the top of the Post Office Tower, and it burned like a candle on a birthday cake.

At least we're getting out of all this, Donna thought. *Away from London.*

Only they didn't leave. Instead, they swooped towards a skyscraper, proud and undamaged in the centre of the city. A helipad the size of a baseball pitch jutted out of the top of it, reaching up as if to catch them in its iron glove. Emblazoned across it was the UNIT logo – clearly they'd stopped hiding in the shadows and were here to protect the world. The helicopter landed neatly on the centre of the logo.

Donna eased the Doctor out of the helicopter and onto the platform. It was a long way down with no safety barrier, but she decided to have feelings about that later. She was worried about the Doctor. He seemed a million miles away, a million years away. And she needed him here and now.

This, all this, was definitely *A Situation*.

An elaborate structure of glass and concrete crowned the roof, with two giant blast doors facing down approaching visitors. The doors rumbled open, and staff and soldiers came hurtling out to greet them. Out in front was Shirley Anne Bingham, UNIT's chief scientific adviser, gliding towards them in her wheelchair. Shirley meant business. Which was odd to say about a scientist, but that was the thing about Shirley. She looked at microscopes to win.

'Oh, here comes trouble,' said Donna.

'I could say the same about you,' smiled Shirley.

And who was the woman striding beside her? Donna had spent most of her life asking to speak to a manager and this woman finally fitted the bill. She was about Donna's age and wore a trouser suit like it was a uniform.

The Doctor snapped out of his reverie. 'Kate Lethbridge-Stewart!' His face lit up. 'I can remember your father working night and day to keep UNIT secret and look at you now! Out and proud and defending the Earth.'

He reached out for a handshake but Kate pushed past and squeezed him in a hug. The Doctor's beam faded when she released him and he saw the desperation in her eyes.

'I've fought them all: robots and insects and Yeti and clones.' Kate stared down at the city burning beneath them. 'But what do we do this time, Doctor? How do we fight the human race?'

Move 4

Welcome to the headquarters of UNIT. Playing at running the world.

The operations room was better than any office Donna had ever been in. It looked more like a spaceship. Shiny desks full of computers that did something, each facing a platform filled with impressive viewscreens that were overseeing creation.

All an illusion.

But games – they are simply illusions with rules.

Donna, having entered UNIT HQ from the helipad, found it all a bit much. All these people doing stuff, some of them in uniforms, some of them in lab coats, some of them in smart office clothes (blimey, were they temps? Which agency supplied them? Because they all looked like models). Oh, and over there, because of course there would be, was a giant android alien thing that – wait, was it growing out of a desk? Did it just wave at her with one of its metallic limbs?

The Doctor ran on ahead like a child entering Whipsnade Zoo. Kate leaned over to Donna. 'Your grandfather's safe, we've built a security zone at the Chiswick Flyover and taken him there. Full protection.'

Donna felt relief but squashed it down, best stern face on. 'Yeah, but it's not just him, is it? I want my whole family safe – my daughter, my husband and –' in for a penny, in for a pound – 'my mum.'

'I'm sorry,' said Kate, looking professionally sincere. 'We've all got families, but we don't have time—'

'No,' Donna insisted. 'Because how did you know where the TARDIS would land? You've been watching my family, which means you owe them and you owe me.' She was playing this one well. 'If the world is falling apart, I want them protected. Right. Now.'

And with that, it was as if Kate's professional kindness warmed up. She beckoned a passing soldier over as if she was summoning a waiter for the special menu. 'If we could – files Noble, Temple, Mott – get them to Chiswick.'

The soldier saluted and ran off.

'Thank you,' said Donna and meant it.

A woman in a jacket and a hurry bustled between the Doctor, Donna and Kate handing each of them a tablet bursting with information. Donna did her best *Seriously Reading A Screen* face. The Doctor pored over his.

'Good, good, good, now what have we got – are these worldwide? Cos I'm gonna need all the statistics and …' He gave the woman a second glance, and the analysis went west. 'Oh, no WAY?!?!'

He seized the woman in a big, massive, laughing hug.

This is new, thought Donna. *So much hugging.*

Words jumped from the Doctor like excited puppies.

'Oh! That is the best news! But what are you ...? Melanie! Hello!'

'Your face!' The woman (Melanie?) stood back from the Doctor and regarded him with bittersweet admiration. Eyes older than her years, tick. Infinite patience, tick. Dressed for a difficult meeting with Armageddon, wow. Bombproof as a seaside donkey? Definitely. Donna knew what was coming next – these two were old friends.

Melanie held up a hand. 'Don't. We'll catch up later, we haven't the time.' She turned to Donna with what was best described as a Whole Body Wink. 'I used to be like you. One of his companions.'

'I wasn't the first redhead?'

'No, that was me,' said Mel proudly.

'Although,' Donna considered, 'don't say companion. Sounds like we park him on the seafront at Weston-super-Mare.' A thought. She turned to Shirley, who looked up from her wheelchair. 'Is "park" rude?'

Shirley wobbled a hand. 'Borderline.'

Kate made a final tap of her tablet and addressed the room. 'Stations, everyone! Gold protocols. The Doctor is in the room. Report!'

That was the point where Donna realised all UNIT had been watching them, waiting for this moment. Kind of like wandering into a pub and realising they're waiting to surprise the person behind you.

Shirley pulled up data from her console. 'Two days ago – an increase in violence worldwide. The same increase in

25

every country and all rising at exactly the same rate.'

On the wall of screens, pictures raged – fires and crowds and fury.

'Every single human being thinks they're right,' said Kate. 'And won't be told otherwise.'

Colonel Ibrahim pulled up a video file. 'That plane crash? The F665 Boston to Heathrow. The pilot declared his right to land wherever he wanted.'

And there was the pilot on screen, giggling in his cockpit. Behind him a frantic hammering on the cockpit door as he laughed straight into the camera. 'I'm coming home! Look out London, Daddy's coming ho—!'

The picture cut off and a chill filled the room.

'But…' The Doctor was working this out slowly. 'If everyone's gone mad…?'

'So has the government,' nodded Kate, pulling up another video.

Prime Minister Edward Lawn Bridges had spent a very large amount of money building the briefing room at Downing Street and then never got round to using it. The Prime Minister had fancied talking to his subjects on a daily basis, but had been steered clear of it for very sensible operational reasons – his advisers had steadily realised that their boss didn't bother hiding his dislike of people unless they owned at least two yachts.

Today was different. Faced with a terrible crisis, the Prime Minister had been forced to address the nation.

And there he was, falling out of his suit and onto the podium, bleary-eyed and scornful, laughing at someone off camera. '… but what do I care? I mean, seriously?' He focused briefly on all those watching. 'Why should I care about *you*?'

Donna shuddered as Kate paused the video on the Prime Minister's sneering face. 'No change there, then.' Donna hadn't voted for him. Her mother had. It had been a tense corned beef Bolognese that night.

'But …' The Doctor was staring in horror at the screen. 'He's got nuclear weapons.'

'We activated UNIT Override One,' said Kate smoothly. 'All nuclear codes in the nine armed countries have been locked away.'

Well played, UNIT. Very well played.

In a bunker underneath a bunker underneath the heart of Washington, a soldier stood impassively at attention. One hand was saluting. The other was holding a bulky black briefcase containing the authorisations and firing codes that could send the world to war: the nuclear football.

A heavy metal door slammed shut, sealing him in a secure chamber.

Six UNIT soldiers stood guard outside, weapons aimed. Ready to defend him with their lives.

'But are they safe? Are they secret?' the Doctor asked.

'That's the problem,' admitted Kate.

In the bunker underneath the bunker, the safest place in the world, there was a knock at the door. The six UNIT soldiers looked up.

The location of the bunker was known to only three people.

And one of them was pounding on the door of their bunker, his face pressed up against the bombproof glass, twisted in fury. The new President of the United States was demanding to play with his toys. And he clearly wasn't about to give up.

Move 5

You are inside the brain of the President of the United States. Can you find your way out?

Move 6

In the Doctor's experience, one madman with a screwdriver and determination could change the world. No matter how secure those weapons, it was only a matter of time. 'How long do you think we've got?' he asked.

'Could be hours. Could be minutes,' Kate admitted.

Donna scowled. 'Minutes?'

A thought struck the Doctor. He turned around, taking in the entire UNIT HQ. 'You're all fine, though. You're all completely normal – and that's because…' His eyes alighted on the armband Kate was wearing. A little silver bracelet with a tiny blue light. Everyone on the floor was wearing one. 'Ah.'

Kate extended her arm, showing it off. 'We call it the Zeedex.'

The android embedded in the desk leaned forward, full of bronze pride. '+++ AN INVENTION OF THE VLINX +++' it purred, bowing slightly.

'Oh hello, the Vlinx!' the Doctor beamed. 'I'm the Doctor. So, why's it called a Zeedex?'

The Vlinx shifted. '+++ GOOD NAME +++' it said, appearing to casually blow dust off a copper knuckle.

'Right,' the Doctor nodded.

'The Zeedex disrupts the brain and flattens the spike,' Kate explained. 'Keeps everything calm.'

'And the spike is...?'

Kate grimaced. 'I think I need to show you.' This move was necessary, but that didn't mean she was going to enjoy it. She crossed over to Shirley's desk, nodding at her scientific adviser grimly. 'Activate brain scan.'

Shirley adjusted her tablet, and a reasonably flat wave pattern appeared on the display screens. Kate pointed to the display screens.

'That's my brain activity. Seems normal. Albeit slightly heightened, given that it's the end of the world.' Kate allowed herself a small smile. 'Now. Keep your eyes on the scan and deactivate my Zeedex. Sorry in advance, everyone.'

Shirley tapped her tablet. The blue light on Kate's armband changed to a red one.

For a moment or two, nothing really happened.

'Well?' asked Kate. A little curt. A touch crisp. Something shifted behind her eyes. The Doctor didn't care for it one bit.

'Um. Hello,' he said.

'Hello,' Kate replied.

'How are you?'

'Fine.'

The waveform continued to march steadily across the screen.

'Busy day?' the Doctor ventured.

'Why'd you want to know?' Kate snapped.

A single red spike appeared in the wavelength.

'Oh, I'm just asking,' the Doctor said. 'Why. Is that a problem?'

And the spike appeared again and again. A series of angry red lines, rising and falling. They looked familiar. His foot tapped involuntarily.

'A problem?' Kate scoffed. 'It's an invasion of my privacy, in fact. It's an assault on my civic rights. And I think –' she whirled around, jabbing a finger at the Doctor – 'it's highly relevant that the person demanding information from me is an alien.'

'Oh-kayyy,' the Doctor glanced at Shirley, who reached forward to gently reactivate the armband. Only Kate was too quick for them both, tearing her Zeedex off and throwing it to the floor.

'I think you'll find I'm in charge here,' she snarled at Shirley, who was clearly taken aback. 'We have been infiltrated! By aliens! By a man with two hearts who changes his face and cannot be trusted. And by –' she advanced on Mel and Donna, fury twisting her features. 'And you and her – both of you with Red Hair. What is this, some sort of conspiracy? Eh? What are you hiding?' She pushed her face forward, waiting for an explanation.

Donna, gobsmacked, seemed speechless for once. Mel awkwardly studied the floor.

Kate dismissed them with a shrug, bearing down on Shirley. 'And as for you – in that chair. I've seen you walk. I've seen you walking around – don't deny it!'

Shirley looked up at Kate, defiant, but tears pricking at her eyes.

Two soldiers appeared either side of Kate and took hold of her. 'Don't!' she cried, fighting them off. 'You can't stop me! It's about time you all heard the truth!'

The soldiers slipped a fresh armband on their struggling boss. For a moment she went rigid and then broke away from them, staggering a couple of steps. She doubled over, like she might be sick.

The Doctor frowned, glancing up at the screen, watching the wavelength go flat again.

'I'm sorry,' said Kate, still staring at the floor.

The Doctor took her gently by the shoulder. 'No, it's okay,' he said.

Kate raised her head and looked at Shirley. 'I'm so sorry.'

'Absolutely no need,' said Shirley, a little too brightly.

Kate turned away, embarrassed and foolish, but pressing on. The world was still ending, despite her feelings. 'It's not just me, it keeps spiking inside every single person's head.'

'So … what?' Donna was still peering at the screen, thinking furiously. 'Does that mean it's being beamed in from outside?'

The Vlinx shifted in its desk, eager to make a point. '+++ NO +++ IT IS ++++ NATURAL +++' it said in its educated purr. '+++ IT IS GENERATED +++ INSIDE THE BRAIN +++'

Wait, Donna frowned some more. If that was the case … 'But not me. Not Grandad.'

'Nor me!' Mel smiled at her, the smile of someone who'd decided right there and then they were going to be great friends. 'I'm wearing a Zeedex just in case, but I've been fine. Well …' She considered. 'No more opinionated than usual.'

'You and me both,' Donna smiled back.

'Oh.' The Doctor took that thought, chewed it then swallowed it. Both of them. Wilf also. 'Maybe travel in the TARDIS puts you out of sync.'

'So.' Donna had done it. She'd solved it. She'd saved the world. 'Can't you just give everyone a Zeedex?'

Kate curled her lip. 'Imagine,' she said.

Her name was Trinity Wells. She'd worked her way up from news anchor to leading political commentator. Millions tuned in every night to hear her coldly and calmly skewer her guests. But tonight, she had a special message for her viewers.

Crawling across her desk, leaning into the camera, she snarled, 'They are using this!' She dangled a bracelet in front of the lens. 'They are using this to control us and monitor us and microwave our brains.' Her words were dripping with disgust. 'I'm anti-Zeedex!'

Move 7

Oh. You shouldn't be here, Donna Noble. You've fallen down a long snake.

Donna blinked, having trouble taking it all in.

This… this had once been her life, and now she was living it again. Fifteen years of packing school lunches and watching boxsets on the sofa and now here she was, once again, standing in the middle of a Top Secret Base as though she belonged there.

Fifteen years of wondering why her mum sometimes looked at her funny in a way different from all the other ways in which she looked at her funny (sort of sad, a bit pitying, but as though whatever disaster was happening was – just this time – Not Donna's Fault). Fifteen years of Gramps trailing off in the middle of a sentence, which she'd always thought was age and she now realised was something different and sadder.

Well, sometimes we have to go the long way round to get where we should be.

So here she was again, Donna Noble. Standing in someone's super shiny base and having to make out that she belonged in order to stop the world ending.

Move 8

The Doctor stared at the wavelength filling the screen, at the peaks and troughs. Oh, he'd nearly got it. His brain sidled up to the shape, strolled around it, mused and couldn't quite grasp it.

'Can we filter this? On the Abacus Scale? Lose the background noise?'

Shirley filtered the wavelength expertly. 'This gives us a strong coherent wave in the Seizure Focus, peaking seven times.' It now resolved into seven clear hills. Each one at different heights.

The Doctor carried on staring at it baffled, trying to work out what could have triggered it two days ago. There'd been a time when he'd have seen a planet-killing waveform and known just what to do with it at a glance. Now, he needed a moment.

He noticed Donna ask for a pen and paper from Mel, and saw her start to trace the waveform on Mel's screen.

'We've been looking for a trigger,' Kate said to the Doctor, pulling up a graphic of a communications satellite orbiting the Earth. 'This. The KOSAT 5. Launched by South Korea. Two days ago.'

Shirley added another image, grainy video from a space telescope. It showed the same satellite sweeping around the Earth. 'Here it is, right now, 36,000 kilometres above us.'

'The world is now 100 per cent online. KOSAT was the final link in the chain,' Kate offered. 'From the highest mountain to the deepest valley on Earth. Everyone is connected. Completely.'

What's in the satellite? the Doctor wondered.

'KOSAT is clean,' Shirley assured him, overlaying various graphics. 'We've checked and double-checked. It's not like the old Archangel Network, there's nothing hidden in the signal.' UNIT, along with the entire country, had been caught out by that, subliminally hypnotised into thinking that an intergalactic criminal mastermind was actually the Prime Minister.

'Doesn't matter,' the Doctor said, picking up a tablet from a desk. 'For the first time in history, everyone has access to this. A screen.'

He stared at the tablet. He stared at the display screen. The wavelength. The satellite. Something else. Nearly. Nearly. La-la-la. His foot tapped again. Why was it doing that?

'What if it's a tune?' Donna's voice cut across the deck. The Doctor gaped at her. 'What?'

Donna held up a piece of paper, going at full speed. 'I know we've only got minutes to live, but give me a second. Cos I spent six months teaching my daughter how to play the recorder until she said, "This is not who I am," and that was the start of a whole other conversation, believe you me, but if you look at those seven peaks, like this …'

And she turned the paper around, showing the five parallel lines she'd drawn. A stave for writing music on. She placed the paper over Mel's tablet and held it up for everyone to see.

'Maybe it's music,' she announced, triumph blazing from her eyes.

Music? The Doctor stared.

Donna nodded.

'That's a classical arpeggio,' Mel offered. 'Middle C an octave higher,' she paused, a little sheepish, took a breath, and then sang. 'La-la-la-LA-lalala.'

La-la-la-LA-lalala

Everyone human shivered, feeling something very old wash over them. Something almost recognised.

'What?' The Doctor frowned, puzzled. 'What is it?'

Kate had walked up to the screen, her fingers running over the peaks. 'Sing that again.'

Mel obliged. 'La-la-la-LA-lalala.'

If – Donna nearly grasped it.

You're onto something, Shirley thought.

Feeling sad, Kate shivered again.

And – 'Oh! I know that tune,' Donna gasped.

She wasn't alone. The music had sent something sparking through the senses of those watching.

'Where do I know that tune from?' Kate asked, also

deeply puzzled. A sudden flash in her brain, just a fragment of Corporal Menzies' hen night, the two brides climbing onto the bar to dance and Kate, younger but always the sensible one, looking at her watch and thinking she must really call a taxi and stop Osgood climbing on top of it this time—

The flash went from her mind, passed to someone else.

La-la-la-LA-lalala

'I've heard it somewhere before.' Shirley had seen the Doctor's foot tap again, had clocked that he'd not realised it. 'What are the notes?'

'C E G, C G E C,' Mel sang them out. 'It's a musical palindrome. But an arpeggio is just straightforward, everyone knows arpeggios.'

Donna nodded, trying to look smart in front of her new friend. Arpeggios. Right.

'It's a very basic tune.' Mel sang it again.

Shirley shuddered, remembering her favourite takeaway at university. What had its name been? She started tapping at her keyboard. 'The question is, why are we reacting to this one?'

'I'm not reacting to it!' the Doctor said, a bit annoyed. 'How about you, the Vlinx?'

'+++ NEGATIVE +++' the android purred.

'So. Just the humans,' the Doctor continued.

'It's just so familiar,' said Donna, 'like it's been buried in my head for years. But what is it?'

'I've found the original,' said Shirley, ashen. She'd done

a reverse search on the sound, and pulled up the result. It wasn't what she was expecting.

An image appeared on the giant display, copied over and over, a grainy, black and white, distorted, blurred picture of a melting head.

'Ha ha ha HA ha ha ha!' said Stooky Bill.

Move 9

Let's play a game. What are the first five words you can see in the grid below?

H	A	H	A	H	A	H	A	H	A
A	H	A	H	A	H	A	H	A	H
H	A	H	A	H	A	H	A	H	A
A	H	A	H	A	H	A	H	A	H
H	A	H	A	H	A	H	A	H	A
A	H	A	H	A	H	A	H	A	H
H	A	H	A	H	A	H	A	H	A
A	H	A	H	A	H	A	H	A	H
H	A	H	A	H	A	H	A	H	A
A	H	A	H	A	H	A	H	A	H

Move 10

The Doctor, Donna and Mel stared in horror at the puppet on the screen, laughing over and over.

'It's not a tune, it's a laugh,' the Doctor breathed, leaning close to the screen as if about to lick it.

'What is that thing?' Donna asked.

Shirley finished scanning the data on her tablet. 'A Stooky Bill puppet. The first face ever to appear on television. Put there by John Logie Baird himself.'

'But –' Donna's favourite word – 'I've never seen him before. So how do I know that laugh?'

The Doctor took in all thirty lines of information, all five frames per second of the image.

'It's as if the very first televised image has been hiding in every screen ever since, sneaking into your head. Carving a wave. And waiting.'

'Hiding, how?' Shirley protested. 'If there was a secret picture hidden inside every television, we'd have found it.'

'Why, because you're so clever?' The Doctor could be rude sometimes. 'What if little Stooky Bill was smarter than you? Imagine if he burned himself into television itself.'

* * *

He had a point. Original televisions used cathode rays which, if the image didn't change, burnt a ghost into the screen. A ghost that haunted every picture. Modern screens? A little bit harder, but there are five dead pixels in the screen you're looking at now. Five dead pixels. Dead or just dark and hiding something? Ha ha ha ha ha.

'He burned himself into every television through that first transmission, and into every picture that's played on telly ever since.' The Doctor produced his sonic screwdriver, using the gadget to amplify the image on screen. 'Every single picture.'

He tapped the display screen with the sonic screwdriver. It flickered, and the image of Stooky Bill appeared on it: clean and sharp and laughing his silent laugh. 'Screen after screen after screen. And every type of screen.'

He raced to a desk, tapped the screen on it.

Ha ha ha HA ha ha ha!

So he tapped the next   *Ha ha ha HA ha ha ha!*

and the next   *Ha ha ha HA ha ha ha!*

and the next   *Ha ha ha HA ha ha ha!*

and   *Ha ha ha HA ha ha ha!*

Ha ha ha HA ha ha ha!

Ha ha ha HA ha ha ha!

Ha ha ha HA ha ha ha! Ha ha ha HA ha ha ha! Ha ha ha HA ha ha ha! Ha ha ha HA ha ha ha!

Until Stooky Bill appeared on every single screen. On every desk, on every tablet, on each giant display.

'Everyone and everywhere…' the Doctor mused, awestruck. 'He's inside them all. Branding his giggle into your brains. Until he had enough screens to be complete.'

He approached the giant displays. No longer a bounce in his step. Solemn, respectful.

'Since the very first existence of television. He's been laughing at the human race. And driving you mad.'

The Doctor raised the sonic, turning the volume of the laugh back on, bringing it up to 11.

And the puppet laughed on – its frozen smile somehow reaching its eyes.

Ha ha ha HA ha ha ha!

Ha ha ha HA ha ha ha!

Ha ha ha HA ha ha ha!

Ha ha ha HA ha ha ha!

Move 11

Kate Lethbridge-Stewart summarised the state of play. 'Something on that scale. Over so many years,' she marvelled. 'Who could do that?'

'The puppet's just a puppet,' the Doctor shrugged. 'We're looking for the puppeteer. And I've got a memory.' That handsome Frenchman danced across his retina. 'I think something is coming back. After a very long time.'

And now he felt fear. The chill creeping down his spine, tapping each bone as it went. Playing a tune.

'But it's not only the giggle. Don't go thinking you've got an excuse. The human race might be clever and bright and brilliant. But it's also savage. And venal. And relentless. All the anger out there on the streets, the lies and the righteousness... That's human. That's you. That's who you are. Using your intelligence to be stupid. Poisoning the world. And hating each other, you've never needed any help with that.' Way to win over the home crowd. Tell them what you really think. 'But today – something else is using your worst attributes. Playing with you. Like... toys.'

You're getting warmer, Doctor.

'Can we take that satellite out?' the Doctor asked.

The atmosphere in the room changed. The Doctor is a man of war when he wants to be. When he has to be. And he had just declared it.

People went back to their desks, pulling up tactical data.

'All missiles are on lockdown,' Kate explained. 'But …' She paused, proudly. 'We've got the Galvanic Beam.'

'What range?' The Doctor wasn't a fan of death rays.

'We can pick off a pebble on the moon. Trouble is, taking out a South Korean satellite will have international consequences.'

'Tricky at the best of times,' said Shirley. And this was not the best of times.

'So we've been waiting for permission,' Kate concluded. Right then. The Doctor stepped up. 'You have my permission.' He had, after all, been President of the Earth in a past life. He'd been the President of several worlds in his time. He'd run away from the stress of it. But if you run far enough you end up back where you started. With people looking to him. Waiting for him to make the tough call. Take responsibility.

So much responsibility.

'Thank you, Doctor,' Kate nodded. For the first time in several days, she smiled. And – because, of course, like any military chief, she had a big red button – she pushed a big red button.

* * *

Outside, the structure of the helipad began to shift and change – vast motors cueing up the weapon stowed away beneath it, preparing the most powerful energy beam on the planet.

Yes, thought Kate Lethbridge-Stewart, maybe I am a Nepo Baby. She'd grown up watching her father save the world. Well, she would have done if he'd ever been around. But he'd been too busy. Saving the world. It had been a strange childhood. Spent waiting for glimpses of him. That tired smile on his face after a long day. Patiently listening to her excited babble about finger painting while he'd been – well, she'd read the files. Gel guards. Axons. Devil Goblins from Neptune.

Once he was down to pick her up from school. Late, of course. She'd been standing alone at the gates, bored as ever, and glancing around to make sure no one saw him roar up in a military jeep. Instead, it had been a yellow clown car driven by a wizard. 'You should never get in cars with strangers,' he'd told her as she'd got in. 'But Alistair's a bit busy.' Funny, hearing her father's name. She pulled the face. She'd spent her whole life being told her father was a bit busy.

They'd roared off down the road, the man next to her smiling and talking and somehow passing her a bag of sweets while holding his hat on his head. 'Little bit of a problem with giant cockroaches and Didcot power station,' the man had laughed. 'Can't be bothered with that. So I said I'd drop you off at Ballet Class. Which I absolutely can, of course.' A pause, and a friendly wickedness lit up his features. 'Or ... we could go dancing with Anna Pavlova?' And that had been the first time Kate Lethbridge-Stewart had met the Doctor. Now she'd inherited the family firm. Holding the world together with duct tape and the most brilliant people she could find. Just in case, this one time, the Doctor didn't turn up and do what he did best.

Save. The. World.

Donna watched the Doctor striding through UNIT HQ, taking charge – order here, setting adjustments there. He and the Vlinx nodded at each other.

That's my Doctor, Donna thought.

The Doctor bent over Shirley's workstation. 'Have we got the exact date Logie Baird made that transmission?'

Shirley pointed to an online encyclopaedia – already working on it. 'Disappointingly vague. Nothing on record. But I'll find it.'

Mel scooted her chair over to join them, working her tablet. 'I fed the KOSAT fake coordinates so it's coming into UK orbit. Within range in three minutes.'

'You're brilliant,' the Doctor said. 'You both are.'

Shirley and Mel exchanged a grin and carried on reshaping civilisation with their keyboards.

The Doctor sat down in a chair, thinking things through.

He watched Mel work, staring so intently at the code dancing across the screen. 'Hello,' he said to her.

'Hi,' she said, still engrossed.

'You look so well,' the Doctor went on. 'But how ...?'

'Oh right, that,' Mel said. Last time the Doctor had seen Mel, he'd been waving her off on a life of adventure with an intergalactic conman and second-hand UFO dealer. 'Quick version. I travelled the stars. And good old Sabalom Glitz, he lived to be a-hundred-and-one. Died falling over a whisky bottle, perfect way to go. He had a great big Viking funeral. And I thought, Well, time to go home, Melanie Bush. So I got a lift off a zingo and came back to Earth.'

'A zingo?' said the Doctor. 'What's a zingo?'

'It's a thing you get a lift off.' Mel had always had a way of rolling her eyes when explaining stuff to him. He'd missed that. 'But then I had to face the one thing I'd been running away from. I've got nothing. My family's all gone, remember?' The Doctor scrolled through his memory. When he'd first met Mel she'd been a computer programmer in Pease Pottage, and that adventure had been a nasty business. 'But anyway, Kate found me and offered me a job.' Turning back to her tablet with a triumphant stab, she called out. 'Galvanic Beam Payload, boarding!'

Outside, the helipad's transformation was complete as the Galvanic Beam locked itself into place – a manned gun turret, about the size of a tank, with crew running into their positions and a gunner sliding into the pilot's chair. Important sirens wailed their warning.

The Earth is defended!

Bless it.

Donna watched the really big gun power up, face pressed against the window. She didn't even realise Kate was there until the woman whispered gently in her ear: 'Good work.'

Despite herself, Donna flinched. How many prime ministers had heard that from Kate shortly before resigning? 'Er ... thank you?'

'Seriously impressive with the music,' Kate confided, smiling just a little. 'If we survive this, you should think about joining UNIT.'

Donna raised her eyebrows. 'How much?'

'Sixty thousand pounds.'

Donna put on her poker face and shook her head. 'One hundred and twenty, plus five weeks' holiday.'

Kate narrowed her eyes, considered. 'Done,' she said and walked away.

Oooh, thought Donna.

The Doctor smiled. Despite the brand-new surroundings, despite the terror outside and the sense of doomsday approaching, he felt almost nostalgic. UNIT HQ was doing what it did best – protecting the Earth.

'Galvanic Beam in position. KOSAT in range in ninety seconds,' called Mel.

The Vlinx reached into its network, backing up and confirming this.

Shirley was flicking through reproductions of ancient paperwork. Found it. 'Doctor, Stooky Bill was televised on October the 2nd, 1925, at 22 Frith Street, Soho, W1D 4RF.'

'Right then!' The Doctor propelled himself out of Kate's chair, surrendering it to her as though she'd asked for it nicely. 'Fire when ready, don't wait for me.' He turned to Colonel Ibrahim – 'TARDIS?'

The Colonel gestured down a corridor. 'She's waiting for you in Suite 17.'

The Doctor ran into a conference suite, Donna following. Both of them looked at the TARDIS, dominating a room full of desks and expensive chairs and conference phones. They charged inside the TARDIS, slammed the door, and vanished into time.

Up a ladder or down a snake?

Move 12

Donna Noble hadn't missed a thing. Her life may have been spent being oblivious to alien invasions and crashing spaceships, but she never missed a small detail in a casual conversation.

'So, what about Mel?'

They were walking down Frith Street a hundred years in the past. And this was what she brought up. Of course she did. Because *#DonnaReasons*.

The Doctor paused. Behind them was the TARDIS, all safely locked up and for once looking as though she belonged in this place and time. To one side was a jeweller's window – oh, nice selection of fob watches. Maybe he'd buy one. Maybe not.

'Mel?' Donna repeated.

'Oh, she's brilliant, isn't she?' The Doctor rammed his hands in his pockets and sniffed the air. Somewhere, 213 metres to the left, was a bakery doing buns.

'Well, yeah.' Donna continued to squeeze the pimple. 'But I just keep thinking – All this time and you never mentioned her?'

'Donna.' The Doctor stopped, leaning against a lamppost. 'I'm a billion years old. If I stood and talked about everyone

I'd ever met, we'd still be in the TARDIS, yapping.'

'So, you talk about no one, ever? You just go charging on?' Donna wasn't letting this go.

'Yes! Because I'm busy. Like now!' The Doctor jerked his head towards whatever was coming their way, and tried out his third most winning smile, the one that said, Come on – adventure!

'You're busy every second of every day. Look at us now, we haven't stopped!'

Donna scored a point there. It had been a long day for the Doctor. There had been a lot of long days lately, several of them spent in the body of Rasputin. The Doctor stopped leaning against the lamppost. It was now holding him up. This, he reflected, was why he didn't do best friends: because they opened his soul like a tin of beans. He was juggling, juggling, always juggling.

But I juggle with worlds, Donna. I juggle with worlds.

Donna pressed on: 'I saw you, Doctor, I got a glimpse inside your mind, and it's like you're staggering – you are staggering along. Maybe that's why your old face came back. Because you're wearing yourself out.'

For a moment, Donna's words hung in the air and creation turned around them. Had the Doctor caught them, maybe things would have ended very differently. Instead his mind was elsewhere – because, his attention had been drawn to the candy brightness of Mr Emporium's Toyshop, standing out against the sullen greyness of the rest of Frith Street.

Not for Mr Emporium the crow-blackness of the passing umbrellas, the murky green of the puddles, the slick grey of the cobbles or the thick soot of London stone. The scarlet cheer of the shop throbbed.

The Doctor had always loved a little shop.

'Stooky Bill might be on Frith Street,' said the Doctor. 'But the question is, where did Stooky Bill come from?'

He crossed the road, pressing his nose up against the window. He watched the trains whizz past, the horses dancing round their carousel, the little drummer drumming, the teddy bear clashing its cymbals, and the spinning grinning heads of dolls.

The Doctor glimpsed a figure – or did he – behind the counter? No. He was gone. Wait. He was back – no, no, he'd dodged again.

Peek-a-boo!

Peek-a-boo!

The Doctor, squinting through the glass, couldn't quite see.

Was that a hand, beckoning from behind the counter?

Was that a face, hidden behind a shelf?

Was that a man, a very handsome man, his face lit up with smiles, a leather apron thrown over a comfortable plaid suit?

Come in Doctor, come in and find out.

The Doctor threw open the door – ting-a-ling went the bell – and marched in.

'Hullo!' I said.

Move 13

It's me! There's no sense in being shy any more. Whoever you think is writing this book, whoever's name is on the cover – ignore them. They're gone. Well – they're here somewhere, in the back of this cupboard, here on this shelf, in this tiny, tiny box – press your ear close – can you hear the SCREAMING?

Yes.

This is my book now.

This is my book, my adventure, my story, my game. And so I'm telling it.

I've been doing a pretty good job so far – but maybe you've spotted me out of the corner of your eye, peeping round the curtains. But I couldn't resist coming on stage now.

After all, this is my grand entrance. Time for my close-up.

Yes, you may want to talk about the way the Doctor strode into my leetle shop, all ready to confront me.

You may want me to tell you the way that Donna strode behind him, his best friend, ready to fight to the death for him.

But let's talk about me, just me, standing there, in my

lovely little shop full of toys, juggling three little balls in the air. Round and round they go.

And I'm staring at the Doctor.

And he's staring back at me. Because finally he knows who I am.

I throw him a ball. He catches it! I throw him another ball. He catches that! I throw him a third ball, and well done him, he catches that too!

And yet I am still juggling three balls. How am I doing that? Magic!

No, don't write letters, don't compose pithy tweets, don't do a seven-hour YouTube video. We have no time for, *'Well, actually...'* any more. Because I decide what's actual.

I carry on juggling and looking at him. I have taken my eye off the ball, but I can afford to. Because you should always greet your opponent. Rules of the game. I keep juggling and throwing balls and juggling as I say:

'Dee boll ist dee first game ever being invented! Stone-Ager-Man, he picked up ein rock! He said oh! Dais ist ein boll!' I can do all the voices, see? 'He throwed de boll und he killed a man, he zed, oh vot fun! Und now eferybody loves dee bolls! Until dee yearh fife billion, ven ze fery last human picks up dee skull of his enemy and says, dat is de final boll of all, ja?'

'Enough!'

It is Donna Noble. She has snatched a ball out of the air.

Well, well, she's no fun. Not yet.

So. I dropped my balls. They fell to the floor and ran away into the corners, squeaking. Fear not, little ones. I shall find you.

I turned to the Doctor's plaything, and I grinned. 'Ahhh, Tonna Noble! I vondered vich one of you had dee bolls.'

She was not impressed. She did not appreciate my joke. But then again, Donna Noble is fearless in shops – she once returned a Christmas Tree in January because she didn't like the leaves.

'Okay, you know my name,' she said. 'But how do you two know each other?'

If she was expecting a story full of merry japes and past explosions, all she got was a curt command from the Doctor.

'Donna, go back to the TARDIS.'

'What?'

'Go. Back. To. The. TARDIS.' The Doctor didn't take his eyes off me. Did not risk it. Not for a second.

'But you never tell me to do that!'

What lovely hair Donna Noble had. How I would enjoy stitching it into place on a doll's head and combing it nice and straight. I would keep Donna Noble on a high shelf in a cabinet so she could watch all my games. I would let her out, once every thousand years – no, once every thousand thousand years – and I would let her play a game.

She was the Doctor's toy. But now she would be mine. I shared a little secret with her. 'Oh, he is recognisink me! Are you not ge-pleased, Herr Doktor to zee me again? After zo many years?'

'Who is he?'

Shall we tell her, Doctor? Shall we?

'The Toymaker,' he said.

Yes.

Forget the title you've had so far – welcome to:

THE TOY-MAKER

AND THE GIGGLE

by ME

Oh, it's fun seeing it like that isn't it? I might get a logo designed later. Something that'll look good on tea towels and jigsaws and bagatelle.

But who is the Toymaker?

Well…

Move 1,024

A long time ago in a universe outside time lived a little boy, and that boy never grew up. He didn't need to. He surrounded himself with toys.

Oh, he loved his toys.

To start with, he had nothing. It was just a void.

But voids are no fun.

Like blank pages they must be filled, and sometimes that's an awful challenge (I am a writer now! See? I get to write things like this).

Sometimes voids are very dark. But don't worry – that darkness never got cold. Never got so cold and dark that the boy cried because he was so cold and alone and afraid. No. The void was lovely.

Especially when… people came to the void! At first they wandered in, finding it of their own free will, but then he began to lure them.

Because they were so much fun to play with.

Like on the last day of term, they brought games with them – a set of cards in a pilot's pocket, a ball, a dice – so many games of chance.

They played together and none of the visitors won. Ever.

No, no, no – the boy never cheated. Never, never, never. But they lost, and so they became toys. Toys to play games with. Toys to play games with other visitors.

One day, the Doctor visited and stayed long enough to play one of the boy's games – he played for the lives of his companions. There was a handsome space pilot called Steven and a sniffing orphan called Dodo (like me, she could also do All The Accents).

The boy made the Doctor play the deadliest game – the Trilogic Puzzle has 1,023 moves, and no one, not even me, has ever understood all the rules (even though I read them, twice!). But the Doctor played – and the Doctor won.

Well, I say 'won'. I would never accuse another player of cheating. But he knows what he did.

After all those years, that lovely void full of toys was all gone. Destroyed.

And the little boy had to start all over again.

Because that boy was lonely, and he had lost all of his toys.

But maybe, just maybe, the little boy would find somewhere else to play.

Somewhere that would take him a very, very long time to get to.

But he was patient.

He knew the invite would come.

Because that boy adored long games. Long complicated games. Including games of ...

REVENGE.

Move 14

'The Toymaker.' The Doctor pointed at me.

I bowed. 'We meet again, Doctor.' It's what you're supposed to say at this point. (Following the rules? See!)

I let the moment between us come to the boil.

Who would blink first? That's a game.

Then, a grin, and zen ... back on viz ze German akzent! 'But sink! If dee boll vas dee very first game, vot voss dee second?'

Pause for effect.

Take one step back.

Then another.

'Hide-und-Seek!'

I took a final step and SVISH! Two red velvet curtains came down, hiding me from view.

The Doctor leapt over the counter, desperate to reach me, tearing down the curtains. But I had gone.

He was faced with a lovely old door, with a very shiny gold handle.

No, Doctor don't ...

Move 15

The Doctor pulled the handle and stepped through the door.

Donna followed him dubiously. This really was just like old times: tearing through dangerous doors and emerging into an even more dangerous...

Corridor. Yup.

The corridor stretched away into infinity. Wood-panelled, ancient oak floorboards, brass wall lamps. Constructed with exquisite taste. Lined with lovely old doors with shiny gold handles.

'No, no, no, no.' The Doctor recognised a trap.

He and Donna turned round, going back through the door – only they found themselves in another identical corridor. No sign of the toyshop.

Donna craned her neck to check.

Yes.

They now had a choice of infinite corridors, each one lined with infinite doors.

'It's bigger than the shop,' said Donna. 'Don't tell me this Toymaker's got his own TARDIS.'

'The TARDIS is an idea the Toymaker would throw away.' The Doctor was stroking the walls, testing them.

'We've stepped inside his Domain. And it's governed by the Rules of Play.'

Donna wrinkled her nose. The Doctor could make any old nonsense sound majestic simply by Capitalising Significant Words.

The Doctor pointed at the doors, picked one, and opened it – into yet another identical corridor.

'Okay, move forward,' he said, and did so.

That was the thing about the Doctor. He carried on. He kept going. When would he break? That was the point of the game.

They stepped into the corridor. Surely it was the same corridor? Donna glanced back at the corridor behind them. If they took another few steps, wouldn't they see themselves walk impossibly into view – wait – wasn't that her shadow? – yes – another step, she'd see herself through the corridor – just one more step – and then the door slammed shut.

Even as a child, impossibilities had made her cross. Her hatred of her childhood nemesis Nerys stemmed from elbow licking. Donna had been furious when she'd learned that it just wasn't possible to lick your own elbow. Even more so when Nerys had swanned into class and declared, 'Oh, but my brother, he can do that.' What brother? Donna had demanded. 'He goes to a different school.' *Yeah.* You had to hand it to Nerys. In order to solve one impossibility, she had invented not just an impossible brother but an entire impossible school.

Well, the Toymaker had invented an impossible world, and the Doctor was sauntering through it. Yeah, she could tell something was stewing in the slow cooker of his soul, but on the surface he was his normal, casually brooding self.

'But how does this even make sense? I've seen some things with you, but they had a sort of logic.' She'd met the Ood and Davros and even the Adipose. And yes, she'd boggled a bit at all of them – alien servants, gliding madman, sentient weight loss – but the thing was, strange as they'd all been, they weren't nonsense. The Daleks built a great big bomb to blow up reality. She'd understood that. It was nuts but it made sense. 'This? This is impossible. How does it exist?'

Donna had executed her move to perfection. Because the Doctor sagged.

Not his body. But his soul sagged.

'That's what unravels me. All the laws I cling to. Gone.' The Doctor picked another door, leading them through into another corridor. Always moving, always carrying on. The Doctor. But there was less spring in his step now. He stared at one of the doors and, just for a moment, it looked as though he'd rather rest his head against it than fling it open. But fling it open he did.

Go through the door. Keep walking. Keep playing.

'Who is this Toymaker?' Donna hated silences. Even the quiet silence as you smiled at each other over a cup of tea. Silence was made to be filled. 'What is he?'

'When I was young, I was so sure of myself,' the Doctor said, leaning back into his own history. 'I made a terrible mistake.'

He reached out, selected a door and went through it. Another choice in an endless life of choices. So many moves. There was bound to be the occasional bad one.

'I let the TARDIS fall into another realm. A hollow. Beneath the Under-Universe. Where science is a game. And all of us are toys.'

His people had always known the Legend of the Toymaker – told to them as children as a myth, a warning, a temptation. The Doctor was a Time Lord – a people who lived within strict laws. There was something so very appealing about a creature that lived by laws completely different to theirs. Especially when the laws of Gallifrey were so boring and the Toymaker's were so exciting.

YES! So very, very exciting! The Doctor had already turned down my advances once before. He thought he'd had a narrow escape. I knew it had been merely an amuse bouche before the prawn cocktail.

'But you escaped?' Donna prompted the Doctor, bringing him back from a thousand years away.

'Yes. I beat the Toymaker. I won his game. But now he's here. He's found his way into reality.'

And now it was time for the main course.

The Doctor threw open one more door, leading them into a sixth corridor, or was it a seventh? How many more would there be?

He stopped on the threshold. Not moving forward, not moving at all.

The fight had gone out of him.

Too soon!

Amazing what could break a man. All those monstrous plans the Doctor had thwarted, all those battlefleets sent to crush him, when really, all it took was doors.

You. Reading this. You're human. Your soul carries around the weight of all your mistakes, your missteps and regrets. It heaves and groans with them. Every morning you wake up knowing that that burden has only grown heavier in the night. Every cross word, every unhelpful email, every heart broken. Unbearable! And you – your lives are so short! Imagine the weight that the Doctor carried. Several thousand years of wrong turns.

All brought to a halt by – shall we count them – yes – six doors!

'I think he's here all because of me. Cos I got clever, didn't I?' Their previous adventure – a lifetime, or hours ago, they'd been trapped in a ship just beyond the furthest reaches of existence. And, in order to protect themselves from an unknowable threat, the Doctor had used ancient laws, written in the base code of creation. Bad move. 'I cast salt at the edge of the universe. I played a game. And let the Toymaker in. An elemental force with the power of a god. Now he's driven the human race mad with a puppet.'

'Yes, but –' Donna's old favourite – 'you always say—'

'Oh, what do I say, what do I say, what do I say?' and the Doctor was shouting at her, at the universe, at himself. 'Cos I'm always so CERTAIN! I'm all… sonic and TARDIS and Time Lord but take that away, take away the toys, and what am I? What am I now?'

He turned to her, and he scared her. The Doctor had scared Donna once before – when she'd seen how far he could go. This time he scared her because he had nowhere to go.

Just a short time ago, she'd thought she'd got her life back, that they'd run again and this time it would be for ever. But instead, that thing, that nagging little ache that had plagued the Doctor… here it was. What was wrong with him. He was full up but running on empty, and he'd reached the end of the road.

'What am I now?' he said. 'I don't know if I can save your life this time.'

'It's not about me,' Donna said quickly.

'Oh, yes, it is.' And he smiled that wonky smile of his.

She smiled back. 'Well, maybe I'll save you, okay?'

He nodded, trying to be as brave as her.

'You big idiot,' she said, nudging him. A fond little shove. That also got him moving again.

They walked on. The Doctor testing doors. Maybe this one. Maybe that one. Donna at his side, lifting him up. She'd done this walk before. Walking Rose to school – on Rose's first day as Rose. That had been the same thing. Trying out doors until one was right to go through.

'Anyway,' she said, more brightly. 'You beat him before.'

'That's the problem. Odds on, it means I will lose next time.'

'No, it doesn't work like that.'

Oh, this Donna. She was fearless! She was taking on not just the last of the Time Lords. She was also taking on me. What did she know of the ancient rules that held creation together? My, my, she didn't care.

'Cos my dad used to say, dice don't know what the dice did last time. Games don't have a memory. Every game starts from scratch. So you should stand an equal chance. okay?'

'I like that. Well said, Dad.' The Doctor paused to turn up the heat on his smile.

For she was right. We're still learning lessons from those we lose. Life goes on. The universe goes on. The game goes on.

Only…

Well – Donna was only *sort of* right. I carve my playing pieces from souls. *My* dice remember.

And they scream.

But anyway, Donna Noble. You do you, boo.

She'd cheered the Doctor up. 'Let's find the right door,' he said, and his smile turned into a grin. 'Faster?'

'Faster!'

And, taking deep breaths, the two of them ran – throwing open door after door, running through them, into corridor after corridor, seven, eight, nine, ten – twenty

– on and on they ran, the Doctor and Donna, together for ever, laughing at the odds – until –

Slam!

The Doctor went through a bit too fast. Donna took a tiny breath before following. Just getting it back together on the threshold. Barely even a pause. But long enough for the door to slam in her face.

That wiped the smile off her clock.

Donna stood there. Horrified. Gasping with exertion but also with a mounting terror. The door was locked and the Doctor was on the other side.

He was shouting – but of course, she couldn't hear him. 'Doctor?'

> 'Donna! Donna! Don't move!
>
> Can you hear me?'

'Doctor? Are you there? Can you hear me?'

> 'Donna?'

'Doctor?'

> 'Just stay there!
>
> I'll try another door!
>
> I'll come back!'

'I'll try another door. Don't move.'

> The Doctor walked away.

Donna walked away.

Move 16

Donna Noble is in a corridor. There are four doors. Which door shall she take?

> *Door One? Go to Move 17*
> *Door Two? Go to Move 19*
> *Door Three? Go to Move 21*
> *Door Four? Go to Move 25*

Move 17

A brave choice. Donna ran through the door. Into yet another corridor.

She looked left and right, calling the Doctor's name. No.

The door slammed behind her and wouldn't open. Of course, it wouldn't. So, accepting her fate, she carried on walking, calling the Doctor's name.

She stopped.

'That's not funny,' she said. Because the Doctor was standing behind her. 'Creeping up on me like that. Not. Funny.'

The Doctor didn't say anything.

She turned round.

No one there.

Funny. She could have sworn that he was standing behind her.

Corridor. Playing tricks.

So she started off again.

And then stopped.

Because the floorboard behind her had creaked.

She turned round.

No one there.

But the floorboard had creaked.

Which was weird. Because she looked down. Thick, heavy carpet.

Fine.

She'd had enough of this.

She marched off, definitely not listening to anything behind her.

Because there was nothing behind her.

Nothing. No one.

She heard another footstep. This time a foot, sinking firmly into the carpet. And again. And again.

She ignored it and kept moving.

'No one there. No one there at all. Just my imagination.'

Now it changed. A soft little *scuffle scuffle scuffle tappity -tap*.

A sound she knew from childhood. From a dozen bored feet outside dance class.

Her imagination was doing a soft shoe shuffle.

Donna whipped round, expecting to see the Toymaker.

Nothing there.

Of course not.

So she marched away.

Not looking back. Not looking back.

And the footsteps didn't follow her. They went silent.

Donna Noble kept walking, walking until the surprise point that the corridor, without seeming to change its shape, turned a corner. As soon as she turned the corner she heard it.

Distant feet, running towards her. Running. Panting. Closing in.

Donna looked around, trying doors. None of them opened. Not one.

The running feet came closer. And she could hear it – not just panting but snarling.

Still no doors opened.

The running turned the corner. And charged towards her.

But she still couldn't see anything. Not even the carpet stirred as those feet raced towards her, the feet of something panting and snarling and laughing hungrily, ready to devour her.

At the last minute, Donna threw up her hand and …

To try and open a door, go to Move 20
To turn and face her fears, go to Move 22

Move 18

Donna ran through the door. Into yet another corridor.

She looked left and right, calling the Doctor's name.

The door slammed behind her and wouldn't open. Of course, it wouldn't.

Just a corridor full of more doors.

She moved off down the endless corridor.

The infinite ceiling seemed to press down on her. The unending carpet stretched away out of sight.

A thought struck her. *Who changed the lightbulbs?*

Donna smiled and walked on, trying a door or two as she went.

Nope. All locked.

She stopped calling out the Doctor's name and instead tried singing to herself for a bit. A tune that had been hanging around her head for a while.

'La la la – lalala la…'

What was that tune?

She stopped singing and chewed it over.

'La la la – lalala la…'

Someone else was singing. An echo of her voice. But with a cruel little laugh in it.

'Hey, stop that!' Donna was having none of it.

The voice stopped.

Quite right. Donna nodded to herself and walked on.

The singing started again.

Donna shivered and reached out for a door. Which one would she choose?

Door One? Go to Move 20
Door Two? Go to Move 7
Door Three? Go to Move 21
Door Four? Go to Move 23

Move 19

Donna ran through the door. Into yet another corridor. A gentle breeze stirred, carrying with it the sound of distant laughter.

There were three doors in front of her.

To try the first door, go to Move 20
To try the second door, go to Move 25
To try the third door, go to Move 21
To try the fourth door, go to Move 18

Move 20

Donna fell through the door, feeling it close behind her as she tumbled breathless into another corridor.

She thumped on the door, more to tell it what she thought of it than anything else.

Then she turned and looked at the corridor.

Wait. Was there an impossible turn in it?

Yes.

That was weird. The corridor stretched away like an optical illusion, but this one also turned left. And every time she took a step – yes – it felt like something had just ducked around that endlessly faraway corner.

She ran towards it, calling out. Was it the Doctor? Was it someone else trapped in this maze?

And, as she ran hopelessly towards the infinitely faraway corner, she realised... the corner was getting closer.

And the closer it got, the more she felt, she knew – there was something waiting around the corner for her.

Donna stopped running.

She stood still.

She listened.

Could she hear something breathing? Could she? No. She was just – she was letting the Toymaker get inside her head.

There was nothing there.

There was absolutely nothing there.

Of course not.

But, Donna Noble, if there's nothing waiting for you round the corner, why don't you go and see?

Just to prove it?

To go round the corner, go to Move 22
To try a door, go to Move 23

Move 21

Shall we take a moment to talk about game theory? After all, you're playing this game, and you think you are cleverer than me. Are you?

No, don't be shy! Every player of the game is conceited, arrogant – they think they can beat the person they're playing against!

Perhaps you had four doors in front of you, and you looked at them. Which one is the correct choice?

The first door? Oh, too easy.

The fourth door? The answer is never going to be the last option.

Which leaves the second and the third. It's going to be

number two, you think. Or three. A clever player will go for two, but a wise one will go for the third door.

Which is what you've done.

Because you're So Smart.

You open the door, you step through.

And what have you stepped into?

Well now, remember: you're trapped in an endless house.

And also remember: the house always wins.

So.

You open the door. You step through.

And there's nothing there.

You turn around. And the door is gone.

Where are you? In darkness. But more than that. It's cold. So cold. Because it has never ever been warm here.

Because this is my home. This is my realm. No matter how I decorate it, no matter how much bright wallpaper and no matter how many fairy lights and no matter how much I fill it with toys smiling smiling smiling… No matter what I do, I can never keep out that cold.

Oh, it's fine to start with. Then it begins to seep through the walls, into the candy-striped wallpaper. Those fairy lights flicker, the smiles start to freeze on the faces of my toys. The cold comes in again.

I can light fires, I can burn every stick of furniture in the nursery, throw all my toys screaming onto the flames but, when I've burnt it all, only the cold remains.

And the cold is very boring.

So I start again. I build a new realm. And for a while it is warm. And then ... Well, here we are.

Go to Move 25
Or, if you don't fancy that, go to Move 26

Move 22

She blinked. All there was in front of her was a door. Had she been expecting something else?

She went through the door.

The door closed behind her.

How long had she been doing this?

She stepped forward, walking down the – red, fabric stuff you put on indoors ground.

Wait. What had happened to her words?

Never mind.

She was fine. She was walking. She was okay.

A thought struck her, and she didn't like it.

Why was she here? *Nope. Nothing.*

What day was it? *Huh. What's a day?*

Fine. Who's the Prime Minister? *Oh, that one's easy – it's thingy.*

OK, then, what was her name? *Can I get back to you on that?*

Names really were a thing she ought to know. Her own especially.

Still. She was fine. She was still walking. She was okay.

Since she could remember the word 'door', she decided to try a door. Which one should she try?

To try the first door, go to Move 25
To try the second door, go to Move 26
To try the third door, go to Move 21
To try the fourth door, go to Move 18

Move 23

That was close! That could have been anything! It could have been a room full of fire, a room full of laughter, a room full of sound. A room full of nothing.

But no.

It was just a corridor. With more doors.

Donna could hear someone singing an oddly familiar tune. So she sang it back to them.

'*La la la – lalala la …*'

The voice stopped singing for a bit, then sang again, this time with fear in the notes.

'*La la la – lalala la …*'

To try and reassure them, Donna sang it back to them,

loudly and happily, just so they knew they weren't alone.

'Hey, stop that!' said the voice.

Donna froze. The voice was her own.

She heard the sound of footsteps – footsteps running away from her.

Donna had had enough of this. She wanted the Doctor. She wanted to see Gramps. She wanted everything to be okay.

Two doors swung open, the hinges laughing as they creaked. It was a horrible sound.

Still. Two doors.

To choose the first door, go to Move 27
To choose the second door, go to Move 25

Move 24

Naughty! You shouldn't be on this move. There's no way of getting to it.

Le gasp! You've been cheating, haven't you?

Tell you what, I think you'd better go to Move 55

Move 25

Donna went through a door into a corridor.

Yadda, yadda, yadda.

She was beginning to get an idea of eternity. As much of an idea of eternity as a mortal human could get.

Your lives are so, so short! Tiny. Trying to explain immortality to you! Oh, the idea.

Imagine you find yourself in darkness with a box of matches to last you all eternity.

Complete darkness.

One box of matches.

The darkness is unbearable.

So you light a match.

The relief!

A tiny bit of light and warmth in an endless realm. You hold the match up until it burns your fingers.

And then the light goes out.

And you're back in the darkness and the cold.

And one match down.

And eternity still to go.

You reach to light another match, just for a few more seconds of precious relief, then stop yourself.

Best not waste them.

Say there's 100 matches in the box.

Well, there's only 99 now.

Perhaps, just perhaps, you'll be able to pace yourself, only light one match every hundred years. Until then, you'll hold the box in your hands, the memory of the joy it brought you.

One match, every hundred years. You can do it.

Wait, that's only going to get you through 10,000 years. And there's a lot of eternity left to go.

You may as well – yes, there we are – turn the box upside down, let them all fall away.

What use are matches?

Maybe you should make a choice. Not that choices matter.

Perhaps you should go to Move 21
Or maybe you could try going to Move 26?

Move 26

Donna went through a door, feeling it close behind her.

For a moment she felt sick and disorientated. Something pulled at the edge of her soul. The distant sounds of children laughing? Or crying?

Why do we play games? she wondered. *What is it about being alive that makes us want to pretend?*

That's all games are.

Pretending at life.

Endlessly.

Until it stops.

She looked around the corridor she was in.

There were two doors.

To choose the first door, go to Move 21
To choose the second door, go to Move 25

Move 27

Donna went through the door, and emerged into... darkness?

No. Wait. She was in an attic. An old and dusty attic with meagre little starlight glinting through the broken skylight. Dust was everywhere, along with a scattering of bric-a-brac, tea chests and old prams.

Was she in a dream?

She stepped on the old sagging floorboards, relieved to feel something other than plush carpet under her feet.

Somewhere in the attic, someone was crying. Definitely not the Doctor.

'Hello?' said Donna. 'Who's that? Where are you?'

She stepped further into the attic, poking around among tattered blankets.

The crying went on.

(Yes, it's okay for you to turn the page, go to Move 28 and find out what the Doctor's been up to. Shoo!)

Move 28

The Doctor went through the door, and emerged into ...
wait, a school room?

Donna?

No Donna.

The deep blue of night filled the room, little shafts of
light picking out nursery items like curios in a museum.
There was a blackboard on an easel facing abandoned
school desks, each one with an inkwell filled with tiny
balls of blotting paper. Vintage.

The Doctor approached the easel and looked at it. No
secret cryptograms in the chalk markings – just the letters
of the alphabet and a smiling face. A smiling face with
devil horns.

The Doctor's attention was taken by the coat pegs on the
wall. Dangling off one of them was a man hung by his collar.
The man was struggling, making an effort to breathe. He
was also trying to free himself from – was it a straitjacket?
No, no – he was tied up with brown paper and string.

'Help me!' said Charles Bannerjee, for it was he.

The Doctor rushed over to the man who'd started all
this, and tried to stop him from choking. 'I'm here, I've
got you, what is it, what happened?'

'I bought… a toy…' Charles croaked the words out. 'And paid… the price.'

A terrible picture formed in the Doctor's mind. The *correct* terrible picture. 'It's okay – I just need to lift you off – are you ready?' He grabbed Charles by the legs and hoisted him up as if he was a rolled carpet, bearing him off the hook and onto his shoulders, gently falling with him down to the floor. Charles landed with a clacking and a rustle of newsprint, the Doctor crouching over him to try and undo the string and rip away the brown paper.

The words came more easily to Charles as he struggled among the coils of string. 'I came back. To the shop. Because I couldn't stop hearing it. The giggle. The giggle in my head.'

So. This was the man, the Doctor figured. He'd come to this toyshop (tick), he'd bought Stooky Bill (tick), and he'd started the entire human race playing my game (tick, tick, tick). The first victim of the giggle.

How ungrateful of me to put him here!

'I know, that's the Toymaker. I can get you out,' the Doctor was saying as he pulled at more of the string. Gosh, there was a lot of string! And who wrapped a parcel in black string? 'What are these?'

He examined the strings in his hands. They weren't just wrapping up this man – they were also connected to something – to… what?

And suddenly the strings were pulled upwards, yanking Charles to his feet, and then onto tiptoe. He dangled there, the strings coming out of his arms and his hands and his legs and his head.

Charles Bannerjee was a puppet.

A wooden body, painted like the suit he'd worn that day, his hands and shoes little bowls of wood, his elbows stiff – but the face, I'd left the face untouched. It was still his face, twisted into a shuddering agony.

'I asked him to stop the giggle,' Charles continued sadly.

It's true! He did. He came back, just as I was closing up the following night. He'd not had a wink of sleep, he said, he could hear the laughter in his head.

'Please make it stop,' he'd begged.

'I will stop it,' I'd told him. *'If you play my game.'*

'But I lost,' intoned Charles in his empty, sad voice.

The Doctor followed the strings up into the ceiling, seeing if they were attached to anything.

But no – there was no ceiling, just a drifting black mass of cloud, into which the strings vanished.

The strings twitched and the puppet jerked, making a slow, pathetic stagger towards the Doctor. Charles's face was pleading, desperate.

'Please.'

Two wooden hands stretched out imploringly and the Doctor backed away, despite himself. Horrified, sad, and ... Oh yes, AFRAID.

'I'll find him,' the Doctor vowed. 'I'll stop him.'

Charles considered this, tilting his wooden head to one

side. 'And now I dance,' he said. 'When he commands. I dance and I prance, but I can never go home again, Doctor.' His head lolled to the other side, the eyes begging emptily at the Time Lord. 'What would Mummy say if she saw me like this? Oh, help me please!'

Tappity-tappity-tap, tappity-tappity-tap! Charles started to dance from side to side, head bumping up and down with each jaunty little step.

Revolted, the Doctor glanced at the ceiling again – those inky black clouds parted, and there I was! Holding the crossbar, tilting and twisting it, the strings snatching Charles up and about, sending him capering back and forth across the floor. Oh I was huge! Huge and looking down like a god at an ant, or a spiteful little boy deciding which of his sister's dolls to dismember.

Tappity-tappity-tap, tappity-tappity-tap! Charles had always enjoyed ballroom dancing. Oh, he remembered that, moving across the dancefloor, so gracefully that all the girls blushed. No more! *Clippy-clop*, Mr Bannerjee!

'Do you like my puppets, Doctor?' I called down to him. 'Do you like my fun? All of them have played and lost – but here's my favourite one!'

A vicious twitch of the crossbar.

The Doctor looked down – and Charles had gone.

Dancing in his place was a puppet of the Doctor – *tappity-tappity-tap!* His little wooden body writhed and wriggled, his face still real, but wearing the fakest of smiles as it chanted:

'I thought I was cle-ver! I thought I was cle-ver!'

The real Doctor – poor little Doctor, sweet little Doctor, bless him! – he turned and ran.

Turned and ran away.

Move 29

Donna moved through the attic, looking for the source of the weeping. Oh, it had an odd feeling to it, this place. Like a ... like a ... oh, that was it!

Overdone Victoriana, furniture just a little bit too large, rooms just a tiny bit small.

A doll's house.

Spot on, Donna.

She reached a corner, under the eaves – the crying was coming from there, a woman sobbing helplessly.

Donna started to reach into the dark, but oh, it was so very dark.

'Are you okay? My name's Donna and I warn you now, if this is a trick, I will kill you.'

The wailing stopped. Something scuttled in the corner and moved. A rat? A wooden rat?

The rattling, clacking continued and something emerged from the darkness. Donna flinched.

Tottering out of the corner came a creature – a doll of a woman, barely even up to Donna's knee – a big sad head on a tiny body, plaster mascara running around her painted weeping eyes. The doll dragged herself piteously towards Donna.

'I'm poor wee Stooky Sue,
I don't know what to do.
I lost my precious hubby,
They threw me in the cubby.'

Had Donna done living dolls before? The Doctor, *ja*! But she had not.

'You're not real.' She backed away from the poor, pitiful, weeping figure.

Perhaps she didn't realise that Stooky Sue had once been real, had once played my games, just like Donna was now.

Imagine, if you will, a funfair. Let's call it *Mister Mystery's Palais du Fun*. At the end of a promenade at the end of its good days. And a family, three young children tugging their parents towards the spinning lights, the fluttering flags, and the brassy cheery of the Wurlitzer organ.

'Can we go in?'

'Pleasepleaseplease!'

'Mu-um! Da-ad!'

Bless those little mites, those lovely little tykes, those silly scamps. Tugging their parents on, each one wrapped up in their dolly wee winter coats, mittens dangling on elastic from the cuffs.

'We want to go in!'

'We want to have fun!'

'We want a go on the games!'

And Mum and Dad gave in, because Mum and Dad always do.

And they found so many games! So much fun! And the cost – well, nothing to pay up front, of course not. At *Mister Mystery's Palais du Fun*, the first go was always free.

Sadly, the first go was the only go you got.

Which reminds me – as Donna is backing away from poor Stooky Sue – where were Sue's children? Where were her kiddywinks? Where were her munchykins?

Oh. Why, if only Donna had looked up, she'd have seen the three Stooky Babbies lowering themselves down on strings. Li'l Ninja Babies.

But Donna wasn't looking. She was staring at Stooky Sue in horror, repeating, 'You're just a doll!'

Stooky Sue looked up, her too-big eyes in her too-big head imploring.

> *'They miss their dear papa,*
> *They seek him near and far,*
> *They miss their kiss goodnight,*
> *They greet in endless night.'*

Donna was mesmerised by the weirdness of it all.

'Mamma!'

The cry startled Donna out of her reverie. She spun round. There they were! Next to her head. Three Stooky Babbies, dangling, tiny wee hands balled into pudgy fists.

And they sprang at her face – pulling at her hair, clawing at her eyes, screaming and wailing and poking their tiny fingers into her mouth.

As Donna fought them off, she felt something sharp sink into her leg. She tried to look down while swatting away a wailing set of baby teeth from her cheek.

It was Stooky Sue, clawing her way up Donna's leg.

> *'Stooky Babbies are so sweet!*
> *Stooky Babbies want to eat!'*

Donna had kind of worked that one out. She pulled one Babby out of her hair, throwing it into a corner, grabbed a second from her ear, tossed it aside, and finally yanked the third Babby away from her eyes. She held it in front of her for a second, shook her head at it, then lobbed it into an old tea chest.

Before she could draw breath, Stooky Sue had reached her neck and was wrapping her wooden arms around Donna's throat, strangling her. Donna gasped at the pressure, surely far greater than such a tiny thing could have applied.

Sue hoisted herself up, using Donna's windpipe as leverage for her feet. Her face was still miserable, apart from her snarling mouth full of tiny, sharpened teeth.

> *'You've seen the widow cry,*
> *And now it's time to die!'*

Donna seemed to be fighting for breath – oh, she was losing, she was going down.

Sue 1, Donna 0.

Only – only Donna was just getting ready for action.

With a supreme effort, she tore Sue off her neck with both hands, and held her away from her, those little arms snapping for her.

Donna breathed gratefully and regarded the struggling Stooky Sue.

'Hello Stooky, my name's Donna.
Now I think that you're a goner.'

Swinging Sue by the ankles, she smacked the doll's face against the wall, over and over, feeling better with every thwack.

Oh, the violence! Applause! Applause!

POP!

Stooky Sue's head came bouncing off and rolled across the floorboards, coming to rest, still sad and now lifeless, in front of her Stooky Babbies.

The Stooky Babbies had regrouped by a tea chest, and were crawling towards Donna. But now they all paused.

Donna had had enough. 'Anything to add? Babbies?'

Donna regarded the Babbies. The Babbies regarded Donna.

And then as one, they scurried back behind their tea chest.

Donna Victorious turned, tossed away the body of Stooky Sue, and headed for the door. She was getting out of here and finding the Doctor.

She opened the door.

The Doctor ran through it.

For a moment, the two players stared at each other, stunned and delighted.

'Oh my god.'

'There you are.'

The Doctor grinned. They'd both been playing games. But they'd found each other – which meant that they'd both won. Right?

That was it.

Toymaker defeated, he'd pack up his Toyroom and crawl back underneath the universe.

We-llllll.

Look again, Doctor, look around you.

Are you in the attic any more?

No?

Then where are you?

Move 30

Da-da-da-da-diddle-da-da-da-da! Now – there were the Doctor and Donna standing, baffled, marvelling at how they came to be in such a lovely huge void staring at a pair of velvet curtains.

But – where were my manners? No seats!

Easily taken care of!

Whoosh! A row of theatre seats came flying out of nowhere and scooped them up, sending them through the velvet curtains, plunging them down, up, down, up, around! Whirling, spinning, loop-de-looping until, with another whisk of velvet, they arrived breathless at—

The Theatre!

Best seats in the house! The only seats in the house!

Their seats screeched to a halt just before they crashed into the stage. And *vot* a stage!

I'd decorated an entire dimension with red velvet. The stage stood resplendent against a lovely painting of the sun and the stars and the heavens all twinkling and smiling – look at the smiling face of Mr Moon. Hello!

The Doctor and Donna stared at it all. I think Donna was impressed, although she was scowling. It was an impressed sort of a scowl. You'll give me that, won't you?

I strode onto the stage and took a bow.

No applause.

As if it had always been there, which it hadn't, I stood over a puppet theatre, a cardboard box with scenery, all dolled up and ready to go.

'Kommensie, ja,' I said. 'Dee show is just beginnink. Vorldvide premiere.'

The Doctor got ready to say something smart, but I wasn't talking to him. I had eyes only for—

'Tonna Noble – zis is for you! Let me tell you vot happened ven dee Doktor, he was leavink you.'

I reached into the puppet theatre and conjured a universe. I lowered in my hands the puppet of an attractive red-headed woman, making her dance between the stars. Well, a paper backdrop of stars on a roller. It was that sort of universe.

'He made eine friend called Amy Pont and he loved Amy Pont – yes, he is likink dee redheads! – und they vent to and fro in time-and-space. BUT! Amy Pont vas touched by dee Veeping Angel …'

I brought up a puppet of a Weeping Angel. You know the Weeping Angels, of course you do, who doesn't know about those lonely assassins, those killer statues. They're terrible at playing games, unless the game is Grandmother's Footsteps. But, anyway, their touch was deadly.

Which meant it was time to bring out the scissors.

'Touched by dee Veeping Angel – so Amy Pont died!'

110

Snick snack, the scissors cut through Amy's strings, and the puppet fell down, through the bottom of the stage and into the beyond.

'She died of old age!' the Doctor protested.

'WELL, THAT'S ALL RIGHT, THEN,' I sneered at him, and brought out the next puppet. A smart, bookish-looking puppet.

'Und den he was meeting Klara!'

At the same time I pedalled the backdrop roller until it showed a quaint street, the sort that looked as though it had lots of sweetie shops. Along the street skipped the puppet Clara Oswald, looking like she owned the world.

'But Klara vos kilt! By a bird!'

And out swooped a puppet of a raven. Behind it, snip-snip went my scissors, and down fell the puppet of Clara.

This wasn't good enough for the Doctor. He squirmed and spoke up: 'She still survives in her last second of life.'

'WELL, THAT'S ALL RIGHT, THEN!' I cried, as I brought out the next puppet. An optimistic young woman jumping along a road full of puddles. 'And den the Doktor met Bill! Not Stooky Bill, but *Lady* Bill! But, alas ...'

And here came the silver, jug-handled scissors.

'She voss kilt by dee Zybamen!'

And snip! Puppet Bill tumbled down.

Again, the Doctor protested: 'But her consciousness survives—'

'WELL, THAT'S ALL RIGHT, THEN!' And I

111

lowered in a host of planets, stars and comets, bringing the space backdrop back round. 'Und den! Dere came dee Flux! Oh, Tonna Noble. Dee poor Doktor – dee Vlux voss killink everysing!'

And my scissors were busy cutting string after string. Down came planets and stars and comets. The planets bounced and then fell still. Some shattered like baubles. Some rolled away never to be seen again. Not a bad representation of the Flux – a celestial hurricane that had devastated half this miserable universe. And all because the Doctor didn't stop it in time.

Oh, my little show had worked. It had annoyed the Doctor. But it had broken Donna Noble. She sat in her chair, looking small and frightened. Had the Doctor really been through all this? Oh, she had caught snatches of his lives since leaving her, when her mind had burned with his, but she had let it go. Let it all go, in a way he never could.

'Is all of this true?' she said.

The Doctor didn't answer her, instead springing to his feet. I thought he was going to rush the stage, or try to hit me. That would have been fun.

No. All that anger, despair, pain, it sank away and he looked at me – so cold.

'I challenge you to a game,' said the Doctor.

Mission Accomplished.

Move 31

Showtime!

I raised one hand, and the puppet theatre scuttled away off the stage. I raised another hand, and there, a green baize card table glided between us. Another snap of my fingers and two chairs appeared, angled so that Donna could watch us play. I wanted her to see this.

I stretched out my hand, and in it was a pack of cards.

'I accept the challenge,' I told him.

'You have no choice.' The Doctor's tone was so grim, I nearly laughed.

But no. This was serious now.

We played for my realm. And my realm was now – (whisper it, children) – not just this planet, but also this universe.

High stakes for a card game.

We sat, two opponents face to face. I flicked a smile at the Doctor as I shuffled the cards, back and forth, taking my time. It is not only dice that remember how they fall. Some of my cards do. Look into their faces and they can tell you what they've been through.

'I came to this universe with such delight.' Shuffle shuffle. 'And I played them all, Doctor. I have toyed

with supernovas and turned galaxies into spinning tops.'
Shuffle shuffle shuffle. 'I gambled with God and made
him a jack-in-the-box. I made a jigsaw out of your history
– did you like it?'

The Doctor frowned. His own history? Wait, did that
mean … oh. Oh. OH!

Let's bring him up to date on his family and friends –
well, to be fair, his oldest enemy. 'The Master was dying
and begged for his life with a final game. And when he
lost, I sealed him for all eternity in my gold tooth.'

I bared my gums, showing off a single gold tooth. I
flicked it with a fingernail. *PING!*

What's that? Did you hear a scream? Just your
imagination.

I shuffled the cards some more, staring deep into the
Doctor's eyes.

'There's only one player I didn't dare face. The One
Who Waits.'

The Doctor frowned. 'Who's that?'

'I saw it. Hiding. And I ran,' I confessed.

'What do you mean?'

He didn't know! Priceless! And I wasn't about to tell
him.

'That is someone else's game,' I said.* And with that, I
laid the cards down on the table.

'What shall we play?'

*See *Doctor Who and the I'm Not Going to Tell You*

114

Move 32

The Doctor reached for the cards, then paused. 'One request.'

Indeed?

'Tell me. The human race, back in the future. Why does everyone think they're right?'

'So that they win!' He could be so stoopid. 'I made every opinion supreme. That's the Game of the twenty-first century, they shout and they type and they cancel…' I dropped into cockney: 'It's awl abaht the banter, dahn't yer fink, Doc? Awl the luverly banter!' I grinned. 'So I fixed it. Now everyone wins.'

'And everyone loses.'

Exactly. 'The never-ending game. Now name your challenge.'

'Simplest game of all.' The Doctor dared to shrug. 'Let's cut.'

'Highest card wins?'

'Aces high.'

I ran through the options. A lovely game. Pick a card. You win if yours is higher than your opponent's. But the beauty of it is that the more you play, the more the odds stay about the same. Clever Doctor. But what has he learned about being Clever?

'I'll go first,' he said, reaching out for a card.

'But he'll cheat!' protested Donna.

We stared at her. Both shocked.

'No.'

'For shame,' I said.

'That's the one thing he won't do,' the Doctor admitted.

'But they're his cards!' Donna wasn't having it. 'He's all tricks! Of course he'll cheat.'

The Doctor gave me a quick I'll-handle-this glance. Be my guest, Doctor – you're already my prisoner!

'The only rules the Toymaker follows are the rules of the game. They bind his entire existence. I win, or I lose, and that's it.'

Well put. I nodded firmly. 'Then play!'

The Doctor reached out, hands hovering over the deck. Glancing up at me – I smiled. Looking back at the cards. A universe summarised in 52 cards. Pick something interesting.

He reached out, and I prayed for an interesting card. A Jack would be a challenge. A Two would be a laugh.

He took the card, held his breath, and turned it over.

An Eight of Clubs. A middling card. All still to play for.

'My turn.'

I reached out, cut the deck and, without even blinking, showed my card.

My old friend: the King of Hearts.

I won.

From here on in, the book is just gloating. If that makes you feel sad, then why not skip ahead? Go to Move 55

If you want to watch the Doctor and Donna experience an eternity of suffering, why not read on? Go to Move 33. *What a cruel soul you are!*

Move 33

I won. Yes. You read that correctly.

Yaroo for me.

'I'm the king,' I told the Doctor, giving the aghast Donna a little wink. 'Und now, meine kleine Doktor, ve vill zee vot is my prize ...'

Oh, the possibilities of having the Doctor as my plaything! What games would we play? What other toys would I make of his precious loves? Who would make him the saddest? Oooooooh—

'One-all,' the Doctor broke in.

Move 34

I will admit, that threw me just a little.

'I won the first game. Many years ago,' the Doctor told me, as if I could ever forget. 'You've won today. Which leaves us equal. And you know that two players are bound by one inviolable rule...'

Oh, how brightly he played a losing hand! I was cornered.

'Best of three,' I conceded.

'Best of three,' he confirmed.

'Then let's make it ... 2023!' I cried.

Why not? Let's go back to the gloriously messy present day and play our final game there.

Let's go out on a showstopper not a book number. Something the delivery boys could whistle.

I reached out, and the velvet that surrounded the room – why, it was all in my hand. SWISH! I pulled it past me, and *piff-paff-puff* I was gone.

The room was less without me in it. Just curtains cheaply painted on the wall which tugged at the building and started to fold in on itself, like a love letter.

Cracks appeared in the ceiling and dust poured down from the rafters. Somewhere deep in the heart of the building, bricks began to howl.

Without me in charge, my toyshop realised it was impossible and ceased to exist.

The Doctor turned to Donna.

'I'm already running!' she assured him.

And the two of them ran, frantic, as the back wall continued to fold in on itself.

Did you know you can only fold the same piece of paper in half seven times otherwise the universe breaks? Well, on the eighth fold, those lovely theatre seats were sucked in, along with the floorboards and the joists.

On the ninth fold, all those spiffy corridors the Doctor and Donna were running through – they got pulled in too, in a splinter of doors and a tearing of carpet and a shattering of light bulbs. Ah, well, guess I'd never have got round to changing them.

On the tenth fold, the Toyshop went – dolls and trains and trucks and skittles and dice all squeezed down from four dimensions to one, my puppets only having time for one final wave before they were gone.

Schwooop!

The Doctor and Donna landed on the wet pavement, ears ringing with the tearing of bells.

There was a missing house in Frith Street, hanging in mid-air, its roof folding down, its ground floor folding up, twisting into a paper fortune teller – four sides, or was it eight or sixteen, each one cluttered with smears of brick and tile and teddy bear, the odd shard of lettering. Ask me anything!

And still it folded and folded and folded, until it was little more than a packet, two inches in size.

Waiting beneath it, as if it had always been there, was a small red toybox, with an open lid.

The packet dropped into it, and the lid of the toybox slammed shut.

Done.

The Doctor and Donna picked themselves up and regarded the toybox.

The street was so quiet. So calm. No one had noticed.

But the universe was still ending.

'He said 2023,' said Donna. 'We'd better get back there.'

'Winner takes all,' confirmed the Doctor.

Move 35

You're the pilot of the Galvanic Beam. It's your job to shoot down the KOSAT satellite which has driven the world mad. Which trajectory will you choose?

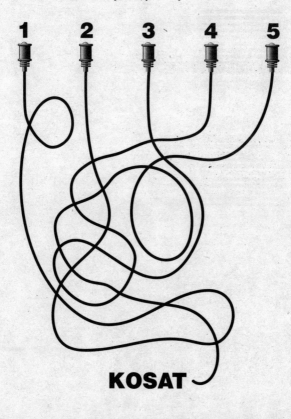

Move 36

A hundred years later and back in 2023 at UNIT HQ the atmosphere was tense. Kate was trying not to show how nervous she was as Mel and Shirley worked through the targeting instructions.

'Accuracy 100 per cent,' said Shirley. 'Satellite within range.'

They watched the beam fire with a force so strong it set the air ablaze. Then they all held their breaths.

Seconds later, the image of the satellite winked out.

'We did it!' Mel shouted.

'Success!' Shirley whooped.

UNIT breathed again. The world was saved. That was, after all, what UNIT did.

Spontaneous applause broke out – just as the Doctor and Donna strolled in. Donna acknowledged it graciously – but the Doctor's face clearly said there was no time for celebration.

That man could literally take charge in a heartbeat.

He was carrying my lovely red toybox. He handed it to Mel, who took it without even raising an eyebrow.

Donna shooed Kate out of her own desk, cracked her fingers and got ready to work. Act like you're important and you always get the best seat at the all-u-can-eat world buffet. Don't hog the prawns, or Donna will end you.

The Doctor was already addressing the room. A battle commander. 'The satellite was only a link in the chain. So, Kate, Donna needs access to the subframe, there is no one in London faster on a keyboard. She's creating a template for this.' He handed a data stick to Shirley, who plugged it into her terminal. 'It coordinates all telescopes and satellites and deep-space scans, across the Earth.'

Shirley nodded, getting to work, filling her screens with So! Many! Numbers!

'And, the Vlinx?' The Doctor turned to the alien, who sprang to attention. 'I need all the mesh reflectors on Earth translated into Digital 5.'

'+++ MESH +++ REFL +++ ECTOR +++ LINK +++' the Vlinx confirmed.

Donna, in a blizzard of data, asked Mel a question. 'Is this static or dynamic?'

'Dynamic. We're using TRIAD.'

Okay, fair enough. Somewhere in her fondue brain, Donna had a grasp both of satellite tracking software and the Beale family tree. Impressive, no? Donna got back to work. 'Gotcha.' After several minutes, she slammed SEND. 'You should all be receiving this – now!'

Data filled Donna's screen then spilled onto everyone else's – an efficient snapshot of the threat the Earth was facing. Look at her go! It'd be terrible to feel just a *leetle* bit smug at a time like this, wouldn't it, Donna Noble?

And yet. Tsk.

Kate Stewart, head of UNIT, saviour of the world, took in the Doctor's expression and the toybox on Mel's desk. 'How bad is it?'

No one stopped working but everyone listened to the Doctor's every word. To them he was a Lord of Time, a spatio-temporal event, and yet, just now he seemed so serious and … small. Whatever was happening?

'Something entered the world in 1925,' said the Doctor. 'But if we're lucky, the program I'm giving you can detect the decay of an energy signature from 98 years ago. Might be on Earth. Might be in orbit. Might be in space. But if we can find the entrance, maybe we can turn it into an exit.'

A door! He was looking for my door. So, it was to be a game of doors!

'What is it?' Kate pressed him. Good for her. 'What are we fighting?'

'An elemental force. Beyond the rules of the universe.'

Smart scientist Shirley was having none of that. 'What's that supposed to mean?'

Mel gave her a sympathetic glance. Good luck getting an answer to that from the Doctor. She'd once fought an interstellar war at a holiday camp on Barry Island. With honey.

Someone was listening to music too loudly on their headphones. She wished they wouldn't. Mel wondered if she was getting old and objectionable and was it time for a tartan shopping trolley? *La la la LA la la la.* Maybe listening to music was keeping someone calm at a time like this. Well, good for them.

The Doctor was trying to explain ME to Kate. Good luck, Studio. 'You think that life is a balance between order and chaos,' he began, 'but the universe is not binary. Far from it. There is order. And chaos.' And everything between. 'And there is play...' He frowned, tailing off as a beat began to build. 'What is that?'

Mel looked around, as did Kate. That music was no longer on headphones. It was playing out of a phone now. She hated that.

La la la LA la la la

'Could you turn that off?' Kate asked.

'Who is that?' Colonel Ibrahim echoed, annoyed, puzzled. A tune he'd heard on a beach at dawn and they'd all been laughing, laughing so hard, luminous body paint catching the sunrise. Chris, Chris, come and dance. But Christofer Ibrahim had turned away and become a soldier. Lovely memory, wasn't it? But why did everyone remember that song?

La *la la LA la la la*

As the music got louder everyone frowned or smiled, each of them having a memory to go with it. Because that melody had been with them for a long time. The Doctor straightened up, looking around in alarm.

'Oh, I think he's here.'

Oh, I think you're right.

And a warning, Doctor, my speakers go up to 11.

Move 37

I promised you a game of doors, didn't I?

I opened a door in reality and stepped into UNIT HQ.
It was the door from my toyshop. All old wood and shiny
gold doorknob and a little ting-a-ling bell.

I'd had an outfit change, by the way. White trousers,
little drummer boy red jacket, shiny hat, and epaulettes.

You can't lead a marching band without epaulettes.

Because …

MUSICAL NUMBER!

Wait. Let me try that again.

MUSICAL NUMBER!

Ahem. Excuse me.

Who are you?

My name is Ms Pockleton. My card.

You can't play with a single card. And I don't understand what you're doing on this page.

I'm a music copyright lawyer. It has come to my attention that you are about to give an unauthorised musical performance of a certain song.

Too right I am, bippy. I've been hiding in that song for decades. And now I'm going to burst out of it. Hold tight!

No. But. Sorry. Have you got the rights to that song?

I created that song.

I'm afraid my clients disagree.

Your clients? Ms Pockleton, cast your eyes over to the train set. See the tiny dolls tied down to the tracks? That's Scary, Ginger, Baby and Sporty. And see who's driving the train? That's Posh.

That's as maybe. But that doesn't change the fact that you've not secured the rights to perform the song on this page.

But I did. When the events I'm currently recounting happened—

I'm concerned about this book. I'm concerned about unauthorised reproduction.

Ooh, get you with your behind-the-bike-sheds talk. Ms Pockleton. I'm an entity from beneath the universe.

And I'm a music copyright lawyer. Just you try putting anything down on this page without clearance and see what happens.

132

But...

Oh.

Yes. Tell you what. You can have the La-La-Las, you've already established those as part of a scale. They're generic. Just don't go overboard.

I'm coming for you, Ms Pockleton. You and I, we shall play a lovely game of Operation. I can't wait to make your ribs buzz.

I shall look forward to it. Good day.

Where were we? Ah yes.

MUSICAL NUMBER!

La-la-la
la-la-la-la!

I sang from my door, twirling my baton.

Then, *ting-a-ling*! From the other end of the room, another door opened. And there I was again. Singing what I'd been singing for a hundred years, songs so cosy the whole human race wore them like a onesie.

La-la
la-la-la!

They turned back – the first door had gone, of course it had. But by the time they turned again – guess what – so had the second door. But, wait, over there, by the Vlinx – was that a door? *Ting-a-ling!*

La-la-la
la-la-la-la!

And another!

La-la
la-la-la!

Ting-a-ling! I'm dancing out of a fifth door! With a cake!

La-la-la
la-la-la-la!

Tut-tut, Shirley, dance along!

*La-la
la-la-la!*

What's through door number
seven?
It's ME!

AAAAAAAAAAAAAAAAAAAAAAAH!

Wait! The eighth door slammed shut! Where did I go? Those nice people of UNIT HQ looked around. A game of doors, a game of doors. Where would I appear next? What was going to happen next? The Doctor hadn't a clue. Because, well, the Doctor had not spent enough of his teenage years in a club called *Kandyman!* Ask Colonel Ibrahim, Doctor. He's got all the moves. (It's what it says on his dating profile, sksksksk.)

Where was door number nine?
Where would the Toymaker
appear next?

*La-la
la-la-la!*

Oh. Hello, Kate Lethbridge-
Stewart. Shall we dance?

And I grabbed her in a waltz,
my face pressed up to hers. I was
smiling, she was – oh – she was
trying to be brave but FAILING.
The look – the rictus grin of a
lower life form as it knows that
it has LOST.

I spun her faster and faster.
Oh, she had moves – *1, 2, 3, 1,
2, 3* – Gorka would have been
proud of her.

*La-la-la
la-la-la-la!*

Her eyes begged me to release
her. So I did. And away she
spun like a little spinning top in
a business suit and BAM! Her
head went right into the wall
with a thud!

Player down, player down!

136

And as everyone stared in horror
at the crumpled figure on the
floor – I vanished.
Was I over here?

Was I over there?
Where would the tenth door be?

Good afternoon, Melanie Bush,
Care to take a turn around the
room?

La-la
la-la-la!

And I grabbed her out of her
chair and I twirled her faster
than my baton, a blur of red hair
and fear, spinning so fast she
was a spinning top. I wasn't even
looking at her. I was looking at
the Doctor and smiling. Telling
him: *Look at what I can do to one
of your own.*

If you hold a butterfly in your
hand, let it go – if it comes back
to you, it is yours for ever. But if
it goes head first into a desk then
maybe it was a rubbish butterfly
all along.

I let Mel go.

Even Colonel Ibrahim couldn't save
Melanie Bush, computer programmer
from Pease Pottage, flying through the
air and crashing into three desks. The
Doctor could have stopped me then –
but he rushed over to her, of course he
did, looking for signs of life in among
the broken chairs and scattered pens.
How dare he ignore *me*?

Look, I was enjoying this. Time for
door eleven!

There is a house in New Orleans!

'Detain him!' ordered Kate Lethbridge-
Stewart, re-entering the game.

And soldiers

'No, don't!' begged the Doctor.

They came striding forwards.
They raised their guns

They call the Rising Sun!*

I just tapped them. With my baton.
Tap! Tap!

**Yes, this is an American folk song of uncertain authorship. You're all right xx Pockleton*

One moment they were soldiers with guns and orders and dreams and ambitions and girlfriends and nanas waiting for them back home along with pet dogs. One did the keto diet, the other loved jam tarts. That was them. In that one moment.

And in the next moment.

Bounce! Bounce!

They were a stack of lovely bouncing balls – big ones, small ones, balls of every colour, toppling and bouncing and rolling and bouncing everywhere.

Bouncy! Bouncy!

One bounced into Shirley's lap. A shiny orange basketball.

She caught it automatically, glanced at it and then recoiled.

Because printed on the ball was a screaming human face.

Shirley threw the ball away in horror.

It's been the ruin of many a poor boy   'Just stop it!'
But I'm not leeestening!   'What happened to
                                    them, Doctor?'
                        'They're dead, I'm sorry, Kate.
                                    Let me talk to him!'

But Kate's first duty was to Ze Planet Urt! She didn't have time for warring gods. She was from a world of guns and flame. 'On my command, open fire!'

It's so easy playing a game against someone with only one move. Bullets? Tut tut.

Every person with a gun at UNIT HQ raised it. Even the Vlinx fired up the lasers built into its eyes.

They slew the Toymaker in a hail of bullets.

They cut me down with lead and fire.

They shot me.

Bang, bang.

My babies shot me down.

Only.

Say it with flowers.

Every time they pulled the trigger no bullet emerged from their guns. Instead, petals and flowers drifted out, flying up into the air and fluttering down! Red lovely rose petals. Carnations! Petunias! Hydrangeas (bit of a squeeze but we'll do it)! Lovely flowers filled the air, along with the scent of summertime. A warm breeze soaked in pollen and the future.

The guards had played their only card. And no matter how much they frowned, how much they shook their guns, all that came out of the barrels were more petals.

Colonel Ibrahim had the fastest, most powerful gun in UNIT's armoury – equipped with Dalekanium tips, half-silver (for werewolves) and half-gold (for Cybermen) – and all it could produce was a shower of tulips.

Kate Lethbridge-Stewart, whose father had shot-up the Kroton Hegemony, raised her own pistol, rage twisting her face and she aimed and she pulled the trigger. Blam! Blam! Blam! A bouquet of roses landed at my feet. I was an opera singer taking my encore!

La-la-la-la-la-la!

More guards ran in with machine guns, spraying the room with cherry blossom!

I danced in a rain of petals.

I rolled around on a carpet of chrysanthemums.

I made a snow angel among the roses.

And the room filled with the scent of new-mown hay. Of dawn.

Oh it had been such fun.

The defenders of the Earth had thrown all they had at me.

And they had lost the game of doors.

Time to go. So –

La-la-la, lalala, la-la-la …!

And

He

Laughed

Until

He

Died.

Ha ha ha ha ha ha ha ha ha ha ha ha!*

---

*We got through it, Pockleton. Now, have I got an electric dancefloor to show you…

I reached into the floor and pulled up a trapdoor that I had only just decided existed, and I dropped through it, taking it with me.

Your move, Doctor. Make your last move.

Move 38

Always leave them wanting more. The silence in the room after I'd gone was magnificent. Just the soft flutter of petals drifting to the ground.

Shared glances of fear. Someone was crying.

Donna went over to Mel, who was sitting up, rubbing her head, and brushing away the remains of Kate's treasured World's Best Dad mug. 'You okay?'

'I'm fine.' Mel sounded amazed. 'I was lucky.'

Kate, still a little unsteady on her feet, was striding towards the Doctor. 'Who is he?'

'The Toymaker.'

'And how does he do … all that?' asked Shirley, lovely practical Shirley.

The Doctor didn't answer. He was done with explanations, he was holding the world together how he always did – with plan upon plan, never stopping. It's said a perpetual motion machine is impossible, but, hey – wow! Look at the last of the Time Lords go. 'The Vlinx, speed up those scans. I need those results. All of you – search the building, he's still here. Where's he gone?'

Always make your opponent angry. That's when they make mistakes.

'But how does he do it?' Shirley pressed on.

The Doctor really wasn't in the mood. 'If I told you he manipulates atoms with the power of thought, would you believe it?'

'And is that what he does?'

'No.'

Shirley got ready to ask another question.

'You can't fight him, Shirley, there's nothing you can do.' The Doctor leaned back against a desk, his teeth tearing at the air. Ever since he'd come back into this body it had been one impossible threat after another. And now this. Did he dare let himself feel helpless? There had to be a way out of this. There had to be a—

Ting-a-ling!

Donna heard it first. Very faint. Coming from – where?

Ting-a-ling! Ting-a-ling! A shop doorbell. A summons for attention.

'Listen!' Donna hissed.

Ting-a-ling! A customer is here!

Ting-a-ling! I'd like to speak to a manager!

'Where's it coming from?' the Doctor looked at the walls, at the floor – or the ceiling? Had I tried the ceiling yet?

'Oh my god,' said Kate.

She was looking outside. Towards the helipad.

It's true. There I was, on the helipad. I looked GORGEOUS. I was dressed in a World War One flying

144

ace outfit – serving the full Biggles. Leathers, goggles, white scarf streaming in a purely imaginary wind. I was leaning against one of my lovely old toyshop doors, pushing it open and shut with my toe.

Ting-a-ling! Ting-a-ling!

Come out and play, Doctor!

But wait, what was I leaning next to?

'He's got the Galvanic Beam,' said Kate.

Move 39

The Doctor came running out to meet me. Ye-es, hon, that's always a show of strength.

I was sat at the controls, strapped in like a pilot ready to go to war. War is such a human game. Complicated rules, goes on too long, loved by families.

The Doctor, oh, he was desperate as he ran.

'*Achtung! Achtung!* Backen-sie!' I hallooed. I swung the gun turret round, aiming it at the top of UNIT tower.

That brought the Doctor to a halt. Along with all his other pieces on the board.

Donna Noble! Kate Lethbridge-Stewart! Shirley Anne Bingham! Melanie Bush! Colonel Ibrahim! Private Cole! Private Forsyth!

All of them stopped as my lovely little pop gun lined up with the glass windows of their office. At all the people inside who had been rubbernecking and now were just looking scared.

Poor pawns.

The Doctor was urging people back – clear the board, clear the board.

'No no no no no, every game is ge-needing an audience, ja?'

The Doctor was having none of it. 'Get back inside,' he told his friends.

And I said, 'Nein.'

Rules are made. Rules are broken. I take pieces.

I fired the Galvanic Beam, shattering an entire side of the UNIT tower, sending everyone inside to the floor as the glass wall splintered, raining down on the Doctor's little pawns as they ran for cover.

Only the Doctor did not give up any ground, shielding his face and waiting until the bootiful tinkling of all ze broken glass fell silent.

So. Just him and me.

I would fire the gun again. He knew I would.

I lifted my goggles and let my gold tooth catch the sun. 'Now, we can all have some fun.'

But Kate Lethbridge-Stewart wasn't shutting up and waiting to be taken. 'Where are my staff? The beam has a pilot and an armourer and ground staff. Where are they?'

'I think they're still falling.'

Move 40

Objects in motion. A bouncing ball. A wooden peg doll. A rattle.

All falling off a very tall building.

The rattle rattled.

The ball rolled.

The peg doll screamed.

Now, it should take two seconds to fall from a tall building. Two horrible, nasty seconds.

But that's according to Isaac Newton's law of mavity.

So long as we're still playing by the rules, we can bend them.

Let's alter one constant of the universe, just a little, just in a tiny little space.

For ball and rattle and peg doll.

Let's slow things down.

Let's let them really get used to their new forms.

Let's let this fall take a minute, a day, one hundred years.

Can Peggy-Doll scream for one hundred years?

Can Bouncy-Ball cry for his Daddykins for that long?

What will happen when Rattle realises that what makes the rattle are not dry boring old beans, but his own teeth?

Let's leave them falling.

Move 41

That had been a good move. Cruel. Effective. *Funny*.

It brought the Doctor to boiling point. He actually yelled at me: 'I don't understand why you're so *small*!'

Ouch. Oh, yeah, that really hit home.

'You can turn bullets into flowers,' the Doctor stormed. 'Think of the good you could do. So tell me why you don't.'

You know how it is with the Doctor? Sometimes he gets things wrong. Forgets himself in the presence of his elders and betters. I looked him full in the eye and let him see just a fraction of my true face. Let the air around us burn with fire and time. I only let him see it. But that didn't stop Private Cole from sobbing.

'You know full well,' I said to the Doctor, 'that this is merely a face concealing a vastness that will never cease. Because your *good* and your *bad* are nothing to me. All that exists is to win, or to lose.'

That put him in his place. That popped him neatly back in his box with the instructions folded on top of the pieces.

I mean, he did say some things, but they were just words. Even if, in that moment, desperate to win, he meant them. He really did.

'And you know, full well,' the Doctor rejoined, 'that I've had many faces, containing something far more. So come with me and leave this tiny world, we can take your games back to the stars. We can play across the cosmos. We can be … celestial.'

Wait. He meant it?

'The Time Lord,' I breathed, 'and the Toymaker?'

The Doctor nodded. 'Infinite games.'

He stretched out his hand. Join him. Should I?

Should I??

Should I???

Move 42

Oh, it was tempting. Take the hand of the Time Lord and run for ever.

And yet.

There were other considerations. I scooted the gun turret around, looking down at the world beneath me. So many pieces still on the board.

Over there, people standing outside a burning building, furiously ordering it not to fall on them.

Half a mile further on, a crowded bus smashing itself into a bollard, over and over, the passengers cheering on the injured driver.

To the left a bit, a window cleaner sitting on his little platform, suspended high in the air, meticulously breaking every pane of a glass skyscraper with a toffee hammer.

Take the second right – two tankers ramming themselves repeatedly into a petrol station until the inevitable happened.

Oh, look! The flaming debris landed near a football game. The team playing on while the onlookers fought furiously with their designer water bottles as clubs.

And on the banks of the Thames, a politician gave a speech. He was reassuring everyone that everything was under control, and that there was no truth to rumours that concentrated industrial chemicals had been released into the river. A bored journalist walked up to him and pushed him in, where he swiftly dissolved.

Welcome to Earth. Welcome to Chaos.

To give all that up?

'I have fallen in love,' I confessed. 'With humanity. This world is the ultimate playground.'

As I spoke I was of course COMPLETELY UNAWARE that Colonel Ibrahim and Private Cole were sneaking up on me. One gentle step at a time

'All the sport, the matches, the medals, the gambling and the anger. And the children – shackled to their bedrooms with their joysticks and their buttons. You make games out of bricks falling upon other bricks, you are exceptional!'

Colonel Ibrahim and Private Cole had taken another step. Then two more. Sneaky-deaky.

'And then there's the mind games,' I went on. 'Oh, and the dating and the ghosting, the deceit and the control, you people make me dizzy! I'm in no hurry to leave this place.'

Colonel Ibrahim and Private Cole were now just feet away. So close they could feel my fire.

What did they take me for? A Weeping Angel? I swung my Galvanic Beam back to face them, saluting. 'We can play Grandma's Footsteps!'

I fired three red bolts at Private Cole's feet, sending him scurrying away.

'Or Off-Ground Touch!'

Three more bolts landed at Ibrahim's feet, two inches higher off the ground, sending him hopping away. I kept firing, watching him leap and dance. Slam it to the left. Shake it to the right. La, la, la, la, la, la ...

'Stop, stop, stop, stop, stop!' yelled the Doctor. Predictable gameplay.

'Shooting ducks. That's a good game! All my leetle ducklinks, ja?'

I assessed the pieces on the board. Time to take one.

I trained the cannon on them in turn, watching how they faced up to the sights. Donna, Kate, Shirley, Cristofer, Private Cole (not him, must learn his first name before I eliminate him), Melanie!

Oh yes. She looked at me, so angry. No, more than angry. Like she had played this game before and she was bored of it. Bored of me. Well. There's an easy cure for boredom! Bye-bye, Melanie, otherwise known as Mel, let's see if you can still scream ...

My finger tightened on the trigger.

The Doctor wasn't impressed. 'Your fight is with me. And you owe me one more ga—'

Actually, never mind. I shot the Doctor.

Move 43

I said I'd remove a player from the board, didn't I?

I set the Doctor on fire. I shot the Galvanic Beam right through him, down onto the deck where those boiling energies spattered and burned the tarmac.

And the Doctor ... well. He didn't explode. He just sort of stood there, finding himself impaled on a pillar of flame. He didn't look as agonised as I'd hoped, more – surprised.

Well, I always like surprise moves. Especially when they're mine and I know what happens next.

I spoke to him, to his horrified friends, all frozen by his greatest defeat: 'I played the first game with one Doctor. I played the second with this Doctor. Therefore, your own rules have decreed that I play the third game ... with the *next* Doctor.'

And I turned the beam off – *schwooop*! As it died, it yanked the Doctor forwards, bringing him to his knees before me. The defeated opponent.

He looked up at me – his victor. And a glow spread over him. This is what Time Lords do. They reset the board by changing bodies. Starting at his fingertips and spreading up through him, rewriting every strand of his body – changing the rules of every fibre.

Fascinating.

He lifted up his hands, staring at them, aghast.

His face was so sad.

How unfair – he'd barely had time to get to know this body again, and yet here it was. Time to bid it goodbye, surrounded by his friends, though none of them dared be with him in his final moments.

Wait. Donna Noble stepped forward. No one ever tells the Queen not to move.

'He's not dying alone,' she said firmly. 'You can do what you like to me –' and I will! – 'but I'm going to be with him.'

'And so am I,' said Mel, putting down my toybox and marching towards me, defiant.

I lifted my goggles and regarded the two women. I could've barbequed them both. And yet, they were performing a ceremony. A situation with rules of its own. I bowed my head, acknowledging their wish. Amused by it.

'Handmaidens,' I said.

They ran to his side, each taking a hand. They were there with him. They were his leave-takers.

He turned to them, smiling and sad.

'It's okay,' said Donna.

'We're here. We've got you.' Mel was as gentle as if she were saying goodbye to a pet.

'Thank you. It's not dying,' the Doctor assured Donna softly.

'I know, but…' Donna had a thought. Best check in with Mel quickly before the life drained out of the Doctor altogether. 'Have you seen this before?'

'No, I missed it,' Mel admitted. 'I was unconscious.'

'Unconscious?'

'Well, the TARDIS was attacked, by the Rani, she was this evil Time Lady, although not evil more like amoral, and she dragged the TARDIS down to this planet called Lakertya—'

'Ahem.' The Doctor cleared his throat meaningfully.

'Sorry.' Mel and Donna focused on him again.

'But this old face, didn't last long, did it?' the Doctor sighed.

'You're going to be someone else,' Mel reassured him, 'and it doesn't matter who. Cos every single one of you is fantastic.'

'I thought I came back to this body for a reason.' He turned to Donna. 'And found you.' He wasn't letting this, wasn't letting himself, go. 'But why?'

The glow spread, burning and melting at the edges of the Doctor's face. Did it really matter now? Come on, Doctor. Get on with it!

'Never mind why,' Donna said to him, quite rightly. 'Just mend yourself and come back fighting fit. Cos the whole world needs you, more than ever.'

The Doctor nodded, accepting. The only person he ever truly listened to, Donna Noble.

Let's say goodbye to this doomed body.

159

'It's time,' he said, stoically. 'Here we go again.' A long pause, a last look at his universe before he said goodbye to it. '*Allons-y ...*'

A little sad laugh before dying, a deep breath, and then he stopped holding back the dams on his regeneration, flooding his body with energy.

Time for a new Doctor.

Flooding his body with ...

Any second.

Flooding his ...

Er.

The Glow stayed there, saturating him but not drowning him.

Why?

Move 44

Why hadn't the Doctor died yet? Well? I was owed an explanation.

Don't just kneel there glowing! Hurry up and regenerate. Go on! The glow was getting brighter – I was sure of it. Wasn't it? Surely it was. Nearly – nearly – almost –

'Um,' said the Doctor.

'What's happening?' asked Donna, gripping his hand fiercely.

The Doctor seemed almost embarrassed. 'Could you … pull?'

'Could I what?'

He turned to Mel, holding his other hand. 'And you.'

'What d'you mean?'

'Pull.'

'Pull?'

He stood, taking them with him as he stretched his arms out.

'Yeah. Pull. Each way.' He indicated his arms.

'What for?'

'I dunno.' The Doctor shrugged a glowing bauble shrug. 'Feels different this time. Ouch. Could you just *pull*?'

'Pull?'

Pull

Pull

Pull

Pull

Pull

'Pull!'

Pull

Pull

Pull

Pull

Pull

As Mel and Donna pulled, the Doctor
split
in
h a l f ,
releasing a ball of pure Time Lord fire.

Poking out of the left of
the flame was the Old
Doctor of a minute ago
– confused and wary,
and his shirt suddenly
missing from under
his jacket. He looked
utterly bewildered and
was staring across in
horror at –

Poking out of the right
of the flame was a New
Doctor! So young!
So handsome!
Born laughing, he was
wearing the old
Doctor's shirt.
And not much else.
Oh dear, will no one
think of the gifs?

'*What?*' said the Old Doctor.
'What?' said Donna.
'Vot?' I said.
'No way!' The New Doctor beamed.

Donna and Mel stepped back – possibly in amazement,
but let's face it, more likely in revulsion. Two Doctors,
but with one torso, one arm each, and somehow sharing
a single set of legs

Oh, this was fascinating.

'But you're me!' said the Old Doctor.

'No, I'm me,' the New Doctor replied, examining his

164

hand, the skin dark against the flame. 'I think I'm really me. Oh, I am – *completely* me. Don't just stand there. Push!'

'Do what?'

'Push!'

They raised each arm and, palm to palm, united they pushed against each other. Out of the glowing mass between them came two more arms.

'Does this work?'

'I don't know!'

As they strained they both burst out laughing – the Old Doctor, it struck me, I'd never seen him laugh. I'd not seen him happy. And now, here they were, shoving and shoving until they broke apart, the glowing energy dissipating, leaving them standing there, panting and exultant and … pat-a-cake, pat-a-cake, make me a Doctor!

Uh-oh.

They were in a winning frame of mind.

The Old Doctor had won the jacket and trousers.

The New Doctor had the prize of the shirt and tie, the boxers, the socks and the shoes.

(Excuse me, I must just go over to the fan fics to see what they made of this. Back in a few hours.)

The Old Doctor and the New grinned at each other.

'Hello?' said the Old Doctor, as puzzled as he was pleased.

The New Doctor threw his arms wide in welcome. 'So good to see you! So good!'

And they hugged.

(To the fan fics again! Back soon.)

The New Doctor stepped away, taking in the situation – me, UNIT HQ, me, London burning, Donna, Mel, Kate, the soldiers, me, Colonel Ibrahim's admirable arms, the Galvanic Beam, me.

The New Doctor was cross. But more dangerous than that. He was smiling.

'Now, someone tell me. What the hell is going on here?'

Move 45

Kate Lethbridge-Stewart had never seen a regeneration. Her father had – he'd told her about it very gravely. His Doctor had gone away to save the Earth from giant spiders, been missing for several months, then fallen out of his TARDIS one day, dying. It hadn't sounded like much fun.

But this – the world in The Biggest Danger Ever, and these two Doctor were standing, giggling.

'Excuse me,' Kate began. 'Sorry, but—'

Shirley spoke for us all: 'How did that happen?'

'Ah,' admitted the Old Doctor.

'Bi-generation!' boomed the New Doctor, trying out the word and loving it. 'I have bi-generated. There's no such thing,' he confided, not caring a jot. 'Bi-generation is supposed to be a myth. But look at me! Myth! Myth! Myth! Mel, what d'you think?'

'I think you're beautiful,' sighed Mel.

'*Still* beautiful,' the Old Doctor prompted.

Mel considered this and looked just slightly at the floor.

'Do you come in a range of colours?' asked Donna.

'Yes!' both Doctors agreed.

Do you know what? I was tired of being ignored. I'd

stood back to let the Doctor die with dignity. And now THIS? What did they think I was, chopped liver?

I reactivated the Galvanic Beam, aiming it at the Old Doctor. Then the New Doctor. Why not both? Could I ask them to stand together? Because I'd worked out something brilliant.

'Behold the Game of the Time Lords.' And I could play it to my advantage. 'A dummy who dies! And doubles! And dies! And doubles! I can play this for a hundred years. I'll have vast meadows of Doctors. Dying over and over again. And I'll never get bored because—'

Both Doctors interrupted me.

'I challenge you to a game,' they said together.

Move 46

This was impossible! This wasn't in the spirit of the rules! This was unfair!

'But there are two of you!'

'I'm the Doctor,' said the Old Doctor.

'And I'm the Doctor,' said the New Doctor.

And they both looked pretty pleased about it.

'According to the rules, you can't say no to a challenge.'

'But that's cheating!' I said.

'How?' both Doctors asked. They even sneaked a little grin at each other, loving how in sympathy they were. Dangerous.

I held up a finger and thought this one through. Had I ever been challenged to a game by two versions of the same person at the same time? No.

Obviously, that was against the rules.

Obviously.

Totally.

Completely.

Wait.

Looking at it, there wasn't actually, technically, anything that spelt this out.

Damn.

'I accept your challenge,' I said brightly and openly and not at all sourly.

I leapt from the gun tower, landing on the ground, looking between the two of them.

Game on.

Move 47

I advanced on the Doctors, one of whom was scooting Mel and Donna out of my way. As if! As if I'd bother with the B-Team when the A-Team was being so thrillingly insulting.

'These moments are a joy,' I beamed. 'When someone thinks they can outwit the maker of the games. Do you think a grand total of ... TWO can cause *me* to shiver? When I played against the Guardians of Time and Space and shrank them into voodoo dolls?'

I let that one sink in. I'd kept the Guardians in a crate for millennia, but of course that had meant nothing to them. So now a seamstress in Kalamazoo had two pin cushions, festooned with her second best pins. One pin cushion was black, one was white and each tapered into a birdlike crest with a howling face.

Yes, I had done that to the Guardians of creation. Was I really going to blink at an impertinent half-dressed anomaly?

'Name your challenge, Doctor.'

The Old Doctor made to open his mouth, but the New one spoke over him, pointing at me. 'You said it. The first game ever.'

'The ball!' agreed the Old Doctor.

I always hate it when they don't play the hits. But, I suppose a classic is a classic.

The first game.

'Catch!' I announced, holding up a bright red ball which had suddenly appeared in my hand. 'Of course, before we begin, there's one thing to remember. It's a simple game, really, but I think—'

Surprise move! I threw the ball at the Old Doctor, catching him off guard.

Somehow his hands slipped around it, skidding along the surface, grappling for it, losing his own centre of balance, oh, just drop it, go on, yesterday's man, game over for you and the universe, just this once – drop

the

ball.

He caught it.

And I heard all those people watching relax.

'Nice,' was all he said, lobbing the ball to the New Doctor. Who threw it back to him.

And they threw it

to

and fro

a few times,

getting a feel

for each other

and liking what they

saw

growing in

                                        confidence
        stepping further apart
                                drawing closer together
            as they threw the ball
                                        to each other
                    back
                            and forth
                    relaxed, wait –
                    LOB!

The New Doctor threw the ball right at me. HARD.
        Was that supposed to be a challenge?
                I invented the ball.
        I caught it easily. Of course, I did.
        And tossed it back to him, casual.

        The New Doctor caught it, not even wincing.
                        Looking me in the eye,
                he tossed the ball from hand to hand.
                        Toying with me. With *me*.
                        The cheek!
                He got ready to spin the ball at me, then –

Oh, wait. What? The Old Doctor scrabbled to
catch the ball suddenly flung his way by the
New Doctor. Fumble. Fumble. Got it –
'Hey! I'm on your side.'

'Oh yes, sorry. Hah!'

'Well, don't forget to—'

He threw it at me. Obvious move.
Another easy catch. And if it seems I nearly
lost my grip, that's a feint by ME.
I am absolutely in control of the situation.
Enough warm-up.
Now let's play for real.
For all mankind.
Keep your eyes on the ball.

The ball

                                                      The throw

                        The catch

The danger

                        Catch

                                                      Catch

Catch

                        Catch

                                                      Catch!

Three people deciding the fate of a planet. While a city
burned beneath us.
And the Doctor's champions stared at us in fear and
alarm.
Willing me to drop it.

Well, let's up the pace a little.

Catch, Doctor! You barely got your fingers to that!

        Catch, Doctor! That'll stop you smiling.

Catch, Doctor! Too easy for you?

        Catch, Doctor! What about now?

    Catch!

          Catch!

Catch!

    CATCH!

          CATCH!

    CATCH!!

CATCH!!!

And the Doctor drops it.
And he falls after it.
Down,
Scrabbling and grabbing.
That weak and tired body.
Letting victory slip through his fingers.
Once again.

Wait. What's that glint in the New Doctor's eye?

Wait. What's that in the New Doctor's hand?

How did he get that ball – surely the other one was still
fumbling with

No, don't look away

Look back at the New Doctor
Keep your eyes on the ball
Where was the

ball?

Oh. Damn.
I missed

it.
The ball sailed past me, past my fingertips.

B… u… c… ……….
o   n   e
d
Bounced.
Went over the edge.
Down into London.

The ball fell and, as it fell, it overtook three other tumbling
objects, winked at them, bounced off the pavement, and

rolled giggling away. It was free! Free at last! Well, until a dog seized it and proudly took its new toy home to be slowly and lovingly torn apart.

Back up on the helipad, the three of us stared at each other. Shared shock. Amazement.

Our look spread to the onlookers.

Was that it?

Well, yeah, dumbos.

'B-but...' I stumbled. Because no.
No no no no no no no.
NO.
I can't have l—
l o —
l o s —
No. Can't say it. Therefore, it didn't happen.

'We won,' said the Old Doctor.
'We did it!' laughed the New Doctor.
Such delight at getting a win under his belt
before he even owned a belt.

'No!' I said, 'I think you'll find—'
And then it came for me.
CRACK!
It was starting.
Ow.

The pain of loss.
Had I ever felt it before?
Not like this.

'Best of three,' said the Doctor. 'And my prize, Toymaker,
is to banish you from existence. FOR EVER.'

Crack! Crack! Crack!
'No but I'm …'
I started to fold in on myself.
'You can't!'
Words and deeds and thoughts
'It's not …'
collapsing
'Please!'
into a tiny box of thoughts and deeds and words.

W	P	L	A	Y	E	R	K	N	O	T	F	A	I	R	N	H	O
W	Q	K	D	X	S	K	E	J	G	P	L	E	A	S	E	E	E
K	T	O	Y	M	A	K	E	R	A	R	B	O	Z	G	U	A	Y
E	M	Y	U	N	F	A	I	R	M	V	K	U	S	O	F	V	A
B	P	M	H	O	W	D	A	R	E	Y	O	U	T	E	N	E	B
E	M	N	T	H	I	S	I	S	N	O	T	O	V	E	R	N	L
T	H	E	O	N	E	W	H	O	W	A	I	T	S	S	L	L	F
W	Y	A	B	O	V	E	X	M	Y	R	E	A	L	M	V	Y	G
E	U	T	R	E	L	E	A	S	E	M	E	M	J	O	K	E	R
E	A	L	W	A	Y	S	W	I	N	N	I	N	G	Q	Q	A	T
N	A	N	S	S	Z	R	V	I	C	T	O	R	Y	P	X	J	V
P	P	B	E	L	O	W	I	W	I	N	N	E	R	V	U	Y	K

178

Folded up into a little, angry space, so small my anger spilled, burning out. Time for one last warning, one last challenge, one last throw:

> 'My legions
> are coming.'

And then I was gone. A tiny little parcel falling into the toybox slid over by Melanie Bush, the lid closing around me with a snap.

End of me.

Move 1 (Go Again!)

The waveform on the big screens in UNIT HQ reached higher and higher – twisting and turning until all of a sudden falling, turning into a long snake – a long snake that went all the way down to 1925. An attic flat in Frith Street.

A mad inventor and his gifted assistant are watching the first television screen showing the first picture.

Of a puppet.

Charles always worried. Even from this distance he could feel the heat coming from the living room lamps. 'We're not going to catch fire, are we?'

'That's why we need Stooky Bill,' John reassured him. 'All those lights. No man could sit underneath that temperature.'

The air began to fill with the smell, first of hot dust, and then of something worse – of burning hair.

Underneath the blazing lamps, the glue of the puppet melted, the varnish began to blister, the paint to bubble.

'If I'm to prove that television works, I'll need a moving image.'

The head of Stooky Bill jerked forward towards them.

The two men took a jump back, then gasped in relief –

the glue holding the jaw together had melted, leaving the puppet's mouth hanging open.

'Gave me quite a shock.' John wiped his forehead. 'Imagine. If he could talk. That wee chap's about to change the world. Imagine what he would say.'

On screen, Stooky Bill stared out. Maybe gaping. Maybe screaming. Maybe laughing.

And then he burst into flames.

Both men gasped. John Logie Baird swore softly, and looked to his assistant. They had a bucket of sand somewhere, didn't they?

But Charles Bannerjee sat, gripped by the picture. Shocked, but somehow hugely relieved. The puppet burning, disintegrating, shuddering as it fell. The first television special effect.

An image of death. And somehow, of release.

Why did he feel as though he'd got his life back?

Move 48

The game may have been over but life went on for Kate Lethbridge-Stewart. A lot had happened, a lot that she still needed to think about (what was the dance she'd performed with the interdimensional entity – a tango or a foxtrot?). But Kate's family business was defending the Earth.

She had to contact her entire Christmas card list – Geneva, the UN, the White House, Number 10, the Silurian Triad, the Zygon Central Milkmaid. She had to make sure that everyone knew that, once again, the world wasn't ending.

Sometimes it seemed that her entire life was spent reassuring powerful people that something approaching normal had been achieved. She dreamed of one day picking up the phone and telling them that the world had actually improved. But that wouldn't be today.

A lot of people had died, some in ways bizarre and horrible. She knew that her troops kept a list in an old binder that had been passed through the ranks over the years. The early entries listed Death by Robot Yeti, Mannequin and Daffodil, and now had to be updated with Death by Beach Ball and the Out-Of-Competition Rhumba. Colonel Ibrahim would bring out the tin mugs and toast the fallen with solemnly brewed cocoa.

The thing she really hated was that she never got to talk about her job outside work. She had a normal life with a normal number of friends with names like Anj and Brian who worked 'in the city' or ran Pilates studios. They would have dinner parties, go on holiday together, meet up for Pre-Christmas Drinks Before It All Goes Mad. Kate knew all about them – listened to problems with their parents, contributed to their children's fundraisers, watched them fall in and out of love, always had a shoulder to cry on and expertly, carefully, avoided telling them anything about her work.

Occasionally, one of them would tell her a corporate secret, about a deal with this or a merger with that or a contracting problem. She'd nod along for the requisite number of minutes, sometimes learning about an alien incursion, mostly just offering sympathy and judicious advice. At the end of it all, they'd tap her on the wrist and say, 'But Kate, what about you?' and she'd just shrug. 'Oh, the usual.' And that would be it. She'd give them all the time they needed and then never ask for anything in return.

Every now and then, she'd crack and start to talk about how she was brokering a fragile peace with the Earth's Original Owners and she was losing sleep about how long it could be maintained. She'd start to explain it all – how the leader of a junta somewhere had broken into a nest to steal ancient weapons to finish a grubby civil war. How she'd had to attend a Silurian funeral then sit down with the leader of the nest and stop him from wiping out an entire country. The words just poured out of her and down the conversational sink. Awkward looks, coughs, nervous silences. 'It's a metaphor, isn't it?' someone would say. 'Oh, you are clever, Kate!'

She could never quite work out what lay behind that misapprehension. At first she'd assumed it was some kind of perception filter cast over the Earth. But after the Flux she'd realised that it was just what humanity did to itself. The skies had burned, the streets had filled with alien soldiers, and, once it was all over, there was a week or two of giving to survivors' charities, a few Controversial Opinion Pieces questioning whether it had really happened, and then a minor royal would do something even more minor, and the entire planet would decide they'd rather talk about that and just Never. Mention. The. Other. Thing. Again. And they were always right.

So, Kate Lethbridge-Stewart picked up the pieces of humanity and put them back together again, all ready for tomorrow's threat.

Onwards.

She strode into HQ, issuing orders. She slipped the Zeedex off her arm and held her breath. When ten seconds passed without a hate crime happening, she noticed everyone else following her cue – faces frowning, glancing around as they took off their devices, checking to make sure they weren't barking at the moon before sliding them into pockets and desk drawers. She resisted the temptation to drop hers in a bin. It was a technological miracle that she'd find in a box one day alongside three old phone chargers and a dead battery. Oh *that*.

At least, she hoped so.

Kate looked around for Mel and realised she was at her side, keeping pace with her, holding the toybox in her hands. 'Take it to the deepest vault and bind it with salt,' Kate ordered. Mel nodded like it was the most ordinary request in the world.

Kate glanced over to Shirley, who was already in the middle of three phone conversations. 'Shirley, tell Geneva we're in full resus, tell every base to follow Green Shoot protocols, full liaison.'

Shirley didn't even nod, just twitched one lip – got it.

Kate noticed a young man sat at his desk, staring blankly ahead. Lost. Right.

Give him something important to do. 'Rudi, I want the names of those staff.' A list of the dead always needed to be compiled.

Yes, the game was over, but for Kate Lethbridge-Stewart life went on.

Move 49

Back out on the Galvanic Beam pad, two impossibilities lingered, momentarily forgotten. Two Doctors. Yesterday's man and Tomorrow's man.

One wearing most of a suit. One wearing pants and socks and a shirt. The New Doctor ran his hands over his body, found a tie, and wondered if he should do it up. Nah, let's leave it like this. Casual.

The Old Doctor walked to the edge of the platform and looked at the city beneath them. Saved but still burning. The fires still going – but smouldering now, not building to an inferno.

Sirens were going, and if you squinted – and he'd always done a good squint – there were survivors in sight. People standing dazed on pavements, wondering what had happened, but also feeling normal.

This being Britain, a few people were apologising to each other vaguely for things that weren't their fault. A delivery guy on a bike was weaving his way through the settling chaos. People rolled their eyes. Someone was checking their phone. A queue was forming at a bus stop. A little old lady was telling someone who didn't care that she thought it would rain.

Normality.

'Hey.' The New Doctor appeared at his side. 'We did it.'

When two (or more) Doctors met, they usually squabbled merrily and saved the universe, spiky as exes on a hen do. Just with fewer inflatable flamingos. But not now. The Old Doctor looked at the New Doctor and saw only kindness in those eyes. Eyes set in a face that said, 'You can say anything to me, it's okay.'

So he did. 'How many people died down there?'

'That's not your fault,' said Donna.

She was standing a little back but still between them. Had she been holding him together ever since they'd met, the Old Doctor wondered? It felt that way. He knew she was just dying to catch his eye in the midst of all this terrible tragedy and nudge him like the best friend she was and say 'I know, right!'

But the Old Doctor could only think of all the death and devastation he'd caused. The Toymaker had shown him, in his puppet theatre – a life full of cut strings and regrets.

'You can't save everyone,' the New Doctor said.

'Why not?' The Old Doctor had never been able to answer this question, and felt that the new guy should have an answer. Something to hear before he died.

Because this was bi-generation. He was a blip. Banquo at the feast, Aunt Mavis outstaying her welcome till Boxing Day. At any moment, he'd start to fade away – wouldn't he? So much left unsaid, so much left undone.

He made to turn away, but the New Doctor wouldn't let him. 'You're exhausted.'

'Yeah,' the Old Doctor admitted. Oh, he could do with a sit-down.

'No.' The laugh left the New Doctor's voice. 'But I mean ... Exhausted. Right down to your soul.'

The Old Doctor didn't even need to think about this to know that it was right. He could only nod. And suddenly he couldn't lift his head back up again.

'Come here,' said the New Doctor, and threw his arms open. 'I've got you. It's okay. I'm here.'

The Old Doctor, so tired, stepped forward, falling into a hug. He felt the arms of his new self wrap around him, felt a kiss drop on the top of his head. He was held. He was home.

So, thought the Old Doctor, this is how it ends. Reabsorbed. Going out tired.

For a moment he ached. He was carrying a burden and it'd go back into his new self.

Poor guy.

Only ... nothing happened.

He was just warm. Welcomed? He was still here.

And he was ... okay?

The Old Doctor and the New Doctor stepped away from each other, sharing a perplexed little smile.

Was this it? All there was?

Donna reached out to both Doctors and led them back indoors. It was chilly out here and she didn't want either of them catching cold. She didn't have time for that.

They headed back inside.

A wind blew across the platform. Glass and ashes and forgotten dreams.

What was that on the edge, lying forgotten?

A gold tooth.

PING!

There was no one on the platform.

And yet, a hand reached out. A woman's hand, nails painted bright red.

The woman picked up the tooth, took it. As she did, there was the faint echo of a chuckle. An old madness that knew, gloriously, that some things never ended. The laughter danced on the wind for a few moments and faded away.

Did the woman smile? We may never know. Perhaps she did.

Move 50

He'd never done this before. Normally, when a Doctor dies, there's not really the space to talk the incoming regeneration through the intricacies of the quantum brakes.

Instead, this go, it seemed there was plenty of time to hand over the keys to his time machine.

Plenty of time.

How much time?

They'd lingered on the threshold of the blue box. This, thought the Old Doctor, might be the last time I get to do this. And the new guy was quivering on the edge, full of puppyish energy. Would he stick his head out of the window as he flew her through the time vortex? Not ruling it in, not ruling it out.

The Old Doctor flung open the doors of his time machine and the New Doctor raced inside.

If the outside of the time machine was just a blue wooden police box, the inside was an optical illusion holding its breath.

The Doctor had not had a chance to get used to his reinvigorated TARDIS. It still had that New Time Machine smell: a scent of pine forests and sunsets, mixed with the caramel tang of old books and dark matter. The control room was a moebius strip of white walkways and staircases, curling back on themselves in leisurely impossible spirals.

At the centre of it all was a pillar of light and buttons. Designed for six people to operate comfortably, and despite many lifetimes of just him at the controls, the ship had never adapted. Maybe the TARDIS liked to watch him throw himself across it like he was playing Twister with Einstein? (Come to think of it, he'd done that, once. Albert had cheated.)

Donna strode in and placed herself between the two of them again, her face a mixture of delight and worry. Was this, the Old Doctor wondered, Supervised Play Time?

When the new guy stopped stroking the walls, there were a few things he needed to be shown. The Old Doctor ran his hands over the controls, pointing out a few changes. 'That's the petrolink shatterfry compensator... Moved from there to there... Hyperdynes. Fluid links, obviously, and... well, y'know. Things.' He petered to a halt. This wasn't his ship anymore. Not really. What if he never operated any of these controls ever again? Never threw the Dematerialisation Switch, never operated the Scanner Screen, never ignored the Fault Locator, never primed the Mandrel Condenser? And yet if he didn't vanish or skulk off to fade away on his own, then there'd be two Doctors in the TARDIS. What was that – a flatshare? No. Wait. A timeshare!

'Um. How's it going to work – you and me?' the Old Doctor asked. 'Cos, it's great. I think. Is it? But how do we both ...?'

Was the New Doctor even listening to him? No, he'd sauntered away through the vast white chamber, his hands jammed firmly in his pockets, which was weird, as he didn't have any pockets. 'One thing you need in this place is a chair.'

Ohhh-kay. The Old Doctor decided to assume this was meant well. 'I'll be all right.'

Bam. The New Doctor swung around, and was beside him, brutally kind. 'You're thin as a pin, love. You've been running on fumes.'

'That's what I keep saying!' Donna had clearly switched sides.

'I'm just ... post bi-generation.' That sounded feeble, even to his own ears.

'It's more than that.' The New Doctor seemed to be looking through him, back to his birth. The Old Doctor risked a glance down at his arms. Were they vanishing? 'The last time you regenerated, on that clifftop, do you know when that was?' Well, that had been – let him think, Daleks, Meep, Newton, Spaceship, Toymaker ...

'Er ...?'

'About 15 hours ago. That's all.'

'Wow.'

'And before that, our whole lifetime,' the New Doctor continued, mercilessly merciful. 'Wearing you ragged. That Doctor who first met the Toymaker never, ever stopped. Put on trial, exiled, Key to Time. All the devastation of Logopolis ...'

The Old Doctor saw them all – running from too many rooms full of severe men in cloaks, running through corridors, running over the dust of alien worlds. Always running, from fireballs and death rays and cruelty, feeling that the universe was falling apart around him; that he was holding it together in his bare hands while he ran; that the thing that was stopping him from tripping and dropping everything, the thing, the *thing* that was keeping him, was his friends.

'Adric,' the new guy said gently.

A friend he'd lost. The Toymaker hadn't mentioned that. The boy who'd tried to save the dinosaurs. So many friends. Please don't list them all. Please don't.

'Adric. River Song. All the people we lost. Sarah Jane has gone. Can you believe that for a second?'

Sarah Jane Smith. It felt like they'd laughed their way from one galaxy to the next, seeing eternity as one shared joke they were in charge of. She'd fought Davros and Cybermen and Sontarans and the Trickster. She was so precious, she'd lived such a great life without him. And somehow he'd thought that she'd go on like him for ever. No matter what body he was in, there she'd be, a touch greyer perhaps, but always there with a sharp question and a smile. But no more.

'I loved her,' the Old Doctor said.

'I loved her,' the New Doctor echoed. 'And Rose.'

Donna's face was wearing her 'it's okay to mention Rose' smile. He'd sometimes worried Donna was jealous of her. Well, obviously not. She'd named her daughter after her. What he'd had with Rose Tyler had been special. He'd escaped the Time War by himself, but Rose had saved him from it. He'd offered her chips at the end of the world, and instead she'd ended up exiled in a different dimension. He knew she was doing brilliantly, but he missed her.

He wanted the New Doctor to stop speaking as every word grew heavier.

'The Time War. The Pandorica. Mavic Chen.' That new head shook in wonder. 'We fought the Gods of Ragnarok and we did not stop for one second to say, What the hell?'

That was true. Sometimes he got the details confused. He'd once spent an entire lifetime playing chess with a god whose name he'd now forgotten. How had that even happened?

The Old Doctor slumped over the console. 'How am I so broken if you're fine?' It sounded like a bleat.

'I'm fine because you fix yourself.' And the New Doctor gripped the old by the shoulders. 'We're Time Lords. We're just doing the rehab out of order.'

Move 51

Five hearts in the TARDIS, and only Donna's was breaking. It was like she could see the Old Doctor, her Doctor, for the first time since he'd come back into her life. They'd been side by side and only now, could she see him, thin as paper. Ever since he'd been reborn, the universe had been tugging at his sleeve, telling him that the game was up.

The game was up.

And the Doctor hadn't seen it yet.

Donna stepped forward, holding out her hand to him. 'He's saying you need to stop.'

The first time she'd met the Doctor, she'd told him to stop. He'd stood there, surrounded by fire and the screams of giant spiders, and back then he'd looked like he could go on burning for ever. Now he was a cheap tealight.

'Stop?' The Old Doctor looked at her, and in his eyes she could see the thousands of years he'd walked. 'I . . . don't know how.'

'Well, I can tell you.' Donna Noble's specialist subject. 'Cos d'you know what I did? While you went flying off in your blue box, Space Man? I stayed in one place and I lived day after day after day.'

The Old Doctor stared at her in horror. 'It would drive me mad.'

'Yes, it does,' Donna admitted. 'And you keep going. That's the adventure. The one adventure you've never had.'

The horror.

''Cos I've worked out what happened. You changed your face, and then you found me. D'you know why?'

'No?'

'To come home.'

There. Simple as that.

The Old Doctor stared at her. He'd never had a home. All those worlds and planets and he'd never lived on any of them. He'd never even been at home on his home planet. And was the TARDIS his home? Really? Or just a comfortable pair of running shoes. Kept him going. Always moving.

Maybe.

The time had come.

To stand still.

'Do you mean …' The Old Doctor glanced over at the New one. 'He flies off?'

Don't say yes, don't say yes.

The New Doctor shrugged. Yes.

'But …' The Old Doctor grasped around, reaching for something that might stop all this, anything. He could feel one heart racing, the other slowing down. 'The TARDIS! I could never let the TARDIS go. Never, it would hurt.'

Donna saw the look that passed between the two

Doctors. Her mum had once told her she was too old for toys, and had made her march down with a black bin bag full of teddies to the jumble sale. *Time for someone else to love them, Donna. You don't need them anymore.* And Donna Noble had stood outside the church hall, in the rain, and watched people coming out, clutching jam and jigsaws, and she'd ached, ached when she'd finally seen a child come racing out, holding her Big Womble, running off to new adventures, unaware of all the times and places the two of them had been.

That. But times a thousand.

Her Gramps had understood.

The Old Doctor, her Doctor, had played the game and had won. But now he had to sacrifice the piece that meant the most to him.

Between one breath and the next, she saw the pleading go from him; the shoulders slump as he accepted his fate.

Time to move on. Time to stop time.

Only, the New Doctor was having none of it.

His smile spilled out of his eyes, and he danced. 'Yeah, *but*!' Rules, what rules? 'Bi-generation has never happened before. So what if… What if… What IF?!'

And he was running – the whole room was running as the New Doctor ran around his TARDIS (oh, it was his now), racing down to the service panel in the floor, and pulling out the most impossible thing in the world.

A hammer. A fairground hammer. Test Your Strength.

A red and white striped candy handle, a big red top.

The New Doctor stared at in delight. Just what he wanted.

Donna stared at it in horror. Was he going to start hitting things with it?

The Old Doctor stared at it in shock. The TARDIS had given this to the new guy. He felt slightly betrayed.

The New Doctor waved the hammer around, conducting an invisible National Orchestra. 'What if the Toymaker's Domain is lingering? Just for a few seconds more we're still in a State of Play. So, maybe ...'

And, whirling the hammer round his head, whooping, he ran outside the TARDIS.

The Old Doctor and Donna shared a glance.

Was I Always Like This?

Yeah. Yeah you were.

Good.

Yeah.

Move 52

He waited for the two of them to come out of the TARDIS before he played his move. The thrilled newborn, jumping from one foot to another in UNIT HQ, flapping a giant hammer like a paper aeroplane. He was aware of what he could be, what he could do.

He was the Doctor.

And he wanted them to see it. His old self, his Donna Noble, his Shirley Anne Bingham, his Melanie Bush. They were all his now, and he was theirs.

Because, say it again, he was the Doctor.

'Watch this, watch! Watch! Watch!' He capered delightedly. 'Stand back, that's it! There! Now! Wish me luck!'

'What for?' the Old Doctor asked.

'We won the game. You got a prize, honey. And. Here. Is. Mine!'

The New Doctor whipped the hammer through the air. A test of strength. It smacked into the TARDIS.

Absurd.

Silly really.

You're reading about a grown man hitting a large blue box with a hammer.

And yet.

Isn't it brilliant?

The New Doctor hit the TARDIS with the hammer …

And much as had happened with the old him and the new him, a second TARDIS jumped out of the first.

DING!

If a large blue box could looked startled, the second box looked extremely startled, settling to the ground like an affronted chicken. Both boxes quivered and shook. *Well, I never*, they seemed to say to each other.

'Ta-daaaaa!' the New Doctor roared with delight.

'That is completely nuts,' Donna said, as if speaking for the universe. Shirley nodded.

The New Doctor stood back, leaning on his big red hammer like Willy Wonka opening a brand-new chocolate factory.

The Old Doctor ran towards the second TARDIS, a grin lighting up his careworn face.

Two Doctors, two TARDISes.

'Oh, look,' said the Old Doctor, opening the doors to the new TARDIS. A ramp slid out of the wooden base. He turned to Shirley. 'That's not bad, you know. Wheelchair accessible.'

If Shirley was impressed, she didn't show it. 'At last. You've finally caught up with the twenty-first century.'

The Old Doctor nudged the ramp back in with his toe as he sauntered inside the second TARDIS, hands in his pockets, excitement contained.

The interior of the second TARDIS was identical. Maybe a shade warmer. Maybe a bit brighter. But the same.

Only. Oh! In the corner was a jukebox.

Nice.

The Old Doctor strode out of the second TARDIS, then strolled back into the original TARDIS.

It was the same as it had been a minute ago. No jukebox, still.

Five minutes ago, there had only been one Time Lord in the universe.

A minute ago, there had only been one TARDIS in the universe.

Well, he thought, smiling. *This is a game changer.*

Move 53

Donna watched as the Old Doctor stepped out of his TARDIS, grinning from ear to ear and from Mel to Shirley. Then he saw that the New Doctor wasn't there among them.

'Where is he?'

Horrified, the Old Doctor ran into the other TARDIS. 'Whoa, whoa, whoa, whoa!'

Donna followed him, to find the New Doctor very much at home among the controls, toying with temporal engineering as a cat with a mouse. 'You weren't going to fly off without saying goodbye, were you?'

'As if I would ever do that!' The New Doctor tore himself away from the controls, throwing his arms wide. 'Come here!'

And he grabbed his former self in a hug. Two in one day. And then he folded Donna into his arms. Blimey, Donna thought. Lucky me.

Then the New Doctor turned his gaze on her, full beam. How could a face so young look so wise?

'Look after him.'

That was all he said to her, but it was a lot. It was 98 per cent a warm blanket of knowing the Old Doctor was in the safest hands in creation, but also 2 per cent that time Donna had sat down with Nerys after she'd started dating Ash Patterson and said, 'If you hurt him, I will paint your car pink.' And Nerys had. And the car hadn't liked it.

'Now, if you don't mind...' The New Doctor stepped away, his arms lingering around them both for just a moment before falling back into the switches and dials, futures and pasts and planets and stars at his fingertips. 'There's a great big universe calling. And I need to get going, old man.'

'Hey!' the Old Doctor said. 'You're the old man. You're older than me.'

The New Doctor looked down at himself as if to say don't be absurd.

'Actually, that's true,' Donna said. 'He's younger than you cos you came after him. So you're the older Doctor.'

'OK.' The New Doctor dismissed facts like a Dalek battlefleet. 'Kid, I love you. Get out.'

And, with a smile, he pressed a single button and the time rotor at the heart of the TARDIS began to rise and fall.

Time to go.

'I'm not doing that again!' Donna grabbed the Old Doctor's hand and they ran.

This wasn't their game any more.

The Old Doctor paused at the door, and looked back. Of course he did.

The New Doctor glanced up from the controls.

The two of them smiled. For just a moment that smile was the centre of the universe.

And then the Old Doctor turned and left.

The Old Doctor stood outside the TARDIS, watching the outer shell quiver and fill up with impossible ancient energy. The lamp on top of it started to flash. A warning. An announcement. On. Off. On. Off. On. Off we go.

'Right then!' He cleared a lump from his throat and put on one last show. 'Don't suppose you've ever seen this, Shirley. I don't see it often myself. Stand by!'

And then the noise began. An army of elephants falling down the eye of a needle. Atoms divorcing angrily. Waves of time crashing on eternity's shore. Hope.

'Where's he going?' asked Mel.

'Everywhere,' said the Doctor.

A wind tore through the room. It didn't come from the door or the windows, but from the very start of creation. And it carried the TARDIS away on it.

'Good luck,' said the Doctor quietly as he stood with his friends and watched the TARDIS fade away.

Move 54

Home. What does home look like?

He could have had a castle, he could have had a mansion, he could have had a beach hut.

Instead, it was quite nice, actually. In the middle of rolling fields and green hills, he could hear the dawn chorus, he could hear the cuckoos call, he could hear the milkman doing his rounds, although Donna assured him it was just the bins being emptied.

He'd touched the stones and felt that the building was right. People had lived here, people had loved here, people had cried and died here, but mostly – mostly in a normal way. It was a home full of the ghosts of lives well lived. When he'd said this, Sylvia had had lots of questions about ghosts, but Donna had assured her (once in the hallway, twice in the en suite, and three times on the drive home) that the Doctor was speaking figuratively. But, sometimes he sat in the greenhouse alone, clearly laughing at someone else's jokes.

When most people buy property, they fall in love with a house and then spend months wondering if they've gone insane as they wait for solicitor this and completion that. But not the Doctor. It had gone so smoothly, he still met the estate agent for coffee by the pond, and, yes, he asked to see photos of all of her dogs.

Tiff had never quite got over the man strolling in with the ad (which she was fairly certain should have still been in the window) and announcing, 'I'd like to buy a house, will this one be all right? It looks happy.'

She'd thought he'd looked a bit tired, maybe he'd gone through a break-up, or a loss. He'd not wanted to know about council tax, parking zones, or catchment areas. He'd asked about the number of bedrooms and which ones got the sun. 'That's good. It's not just my house, you see, it's sort of for friends too.' Ah. A dodgy student landlord. Pity. He didn't seem the type. He'd then really startled her when he said, 'And does it have a corridor? I think I'd like one of those.' She'd pointed to one on the plans, and he'd grinned.

'Oh, that'll do,' he'd said, and he'd reached for his wallet. She'd asked him what he was doing. Paying, he'd said. He handed her two twenty pound notes, then, seeing the look on her face, handed over another one, and said he wasn't that fussed about change.

Fearing a prank, or, wondering again about the sad wildness in his eyes, she'd tapped the advert, ran a fingernail under the rather large number on it, and, with forced professionalism, explained it was a fair price but the owner might be willing to negotiate. 'Why would I negotiate? Are they a battlefleet?' He'd made her repeat the sum. 'Is that a lot?' he'd asked. Perhaps, if he was serious, he would like to speak to their mortgage adviser, if he was serious, that was. If he was serious. He'd said: 'Mortgage? Oh no. The word means *death pledge*. Who'd want one of those?' Then he'd asked if he could go outside to make a phone call. Which would have been fine, only he'd taken the phone off her desk, standing outside with the cable trailing in. He talked for a bit, then wandered back in, placing most of the phone on her desk then some of it in his pocket.

'That'll be fine,' he'd said. What did that mean? 'The – money. Oh, I worked for some people for a few years back in the, back in the, well, a while ago, and it turns out... They *paid* me!' He beamed, as though trying out new words for size. 'I did say not to, but they said there'd be a lot of forms otherwise, so I thought no more about it. Anyway, it's all been sat in a bank account. Turns out I'm rich!' He shrugged. He tapped the sum on the advert. 'So this won't be a problem. So. Can I have the keys?'

She was just beginning to explain that it wouldn't be quite that simple when she found herself handing him the keys and saying, 'Just this once.' (From that moment on, the office referred to her as Just This Once Tiff.) She said there'd be some forms to fill in, but he could pop back in later. As he turned to go, he said, 'By the way, it turns out I have a pension. That's even more money, I suppose? They give them out when people turn 66. How silly. That's no age, no age at all.'

Which was why Tiff enjoyed meeting him for coffee by the pond.

211

He'd not lied about friends moving in. There was Donna and Shaun, of course, and their daughter Rose – they still had a place in London, but they didn't mention it as much as the other people around here who were always popping back up to town. Then there was Sylvia, who was Donna's mum, and helped out with the teas at the Scout Hut, whether she was needed or not. Most of all, there was Wilfred Mott. He got the Sun Room on the ground floor. The Doctor had been very specific about that.

Everyone was very pleased to have Wilfred Mott around.

People walking past had noticed one curious thing. There was a new shed in the garden, but only most of the time.

It was a nice day, so they were eating in the garden. Donna had brought out the best china, and Sylvia had taken half of it back in. Sylvia was doing her tuna masala pasta bake, whether anyone wanted it or not, but that was okay because everyone was cooking something. Well, apart from the Doctor – not after the fire station had pleaded with them not to let him near the toaster again.

The Doctor sat at one side of the lovely old table. He said it had once been a tree, until it fell down in a storm, and had then been part of a ship carrying spices, and then, when the ship's captain grew tired, he'd had it made into the table, which had served him well until he'd died and then it had sat forgotten in a barn. Until the Doctor had brought it back into the sunlight.

The Doctor was happy. He was happy a lot lately. The only bit of potential trouble had come when he'd asked Sylvia why she called those things you wipe your hands on at meals serviettes if they went in napkin rings. But she'd simply gone inside to add a bit more salad cream to the tuna masala, to give it that authentic creamy feel.

It was a good day among many good days. So he decided he may as well tell Rose and Donna a story.

As he embarked on his tale, Shaun, handsome and happy in an old jumper, plonked two pots down on the table, while his daughter reached around to pour herself some more juice.

'The cast-iron pot is the vegan, and the one with the flowers is the chicken,' Shaun explained, then frowned. 'I think.'

Sylvia slid more pots among the poppadoms, lifting the lid off one with a flourish. 'Cauliflower cheese. Which doesn't really go with anything, but it was there ...'

Donna shushed her. 'No, hush, it's the eyebrows story.'

'So, this species communicated with their eyebrows,' the Doctor was saying. 'And I thought, I can do that.'

They all smiled at this, as they always did.

'So I stood there, on this clifftop and went –' stern eyebrow waggle – 'I mean you no harm. I come in peace. I am your friend—'

Just then, Mel came through the conservatory doors,

carrying a dish. 'Am I late? Sorry!' She plonked a crumble down on the table, and the air filled with the smell of sweetness and apples. 'The door was open, you don't mind?'

Sylvia patted an old garden chair with sunflowers painted on it. 'Oh, you're family, darling. Sit down.'

'Did you drive?' asked the Doctor.

'No, I got a lift off a zingo!'

And they all laughed. As they always did.

'So.' The Doctor resumed his story. 'She looks at me, the Warrior Queen of the Felooth. And she says –' his eyebrows waggled – 'Good. Now you will marry me? And I said whaaaat?' And his eyebrows shot up. 'And she pushed me off the cliff.'

And they roared with laughter. As they always did.

'Is that true, though?' Sylvia asked. 'Is that really true?'

'We could always go in the TARDIS and find out,' suggested Rose slyly.

Uproar! Sylvia was outraged, and Shaun adopted his most Dad tone. 'You are grounded!'

'Until the Doctor's better.' Donna wagged a finger made for wagging. 'Don't you go sneaking off to Mars.'

'Again,' said Rose with a very straight face.

Donna and Shaun stared at each other in horror.

'No.' The Doctor didn't look up from the mango chutney. 'It's just … the once.' Then he smirked at Rose. 'Oh, you're in trouble.'

'He took me to New York last week,' put in Mel.

'Me-el!' the Doctor groaned.

'The Gilded Age, it was amazing,' Mel continued happily, helping herself to a spicy paratha.

'No, but really,' Shaun said, sternly. 'I know you keep slipping off, cos that box makes a noise like a hundred elephants—'

'No, that's Mum,' said Donna, and Sylvia tutted.

'But Rose is only sixteen. When she's eighteen, we can talk about it, okay?'

'Understood,' the Doctor nodded, serious. 'Sorry. I just can't turn down my favourite niece.'

Rose giggled. 'Ahh, niece. I like that!'

'Well, that's what you are. Along with –' the Doctor looked round the table from Donna to Shaun to Sylvia – 'my best friend, my brother-in-law, and the evil stepmother.'

Sylvia pointed a fork at the Doctor. 'I have barely begun.'

'And mad Aunty Mel!' the Doctor laughed.

Mel laughed back at him, just as happy as when they fled from the Bannermen Fleet on a motorbike. 'Mad Aunty Mel!' She raised her glass in in a toast.

The Doctor looked round the table. What a perfect day. What a perfect life.

Only – someone was missing.

'Grandad. Where is he?'

Oh. Sylvia had the answer. She always did. 'He's off shooting moles.'

And they all looked up – there at the end of the lawn, went Wilfred Mott in his wheelchair, whizzing past, holding an ancient shotgun made in Birmingham. His excited cries drifted over to them. 'I'll get 'em! Don't you worry, Doctor. You stay there! I'll get the little …'

'Leave them alone!' Rose called.

'I will never surrender!' Wilf roared back, buzzing away towards the orangery.

They all watched him go, gliding into the sunlight.

'Don't worry,' the Doctor said gently. 'I gave the moles a forcefield. Love the moles.'

'Wait,' Donna scowled. 'You love the moles?'

'I love them,' the Doctor replied, simply and firmly. 'But here we are—' Another distant gunshot. 'Grandad and all of us. Who'd have thought? I ended up with a family.'

The happy moment settled over the happy day. The Noble-Temple-Doctors. Sat around enjoying good company, good weather, and good food.

'Oh my god,' groaned Shaun. 'I got it wrong! The vegan is the one in the flowers!'

Rose stared in horror at her plate. 'Gaaah! What am I eating?'

Chaos and confusion. The Doctor wondered if this was the worst thing that was going to happen today, as they fussed and changed bowls, Sylvia saying, 'It doesn't matter' over and over again, and Mel quietly swapping Rose's plate for hers.

In among the confusion, Donna leaned over, taking the Doctor's hand.

'You don't have to stay for ever.'

'We'll see,' the Doctor said.

Both their eyes drifted over to the blue wooden box, refusing to gather dust next to the potting shed. 'Do you miss it, though, out there?'

And the Doctor let go of Donna's hand, leaning back in his chair, stretching out, his limbs feeling the warmth of the sun. 'Funny thing is, I fought all those battles, for all of those years, and now I know what for.' He smiled. '*This.*'

The Doctor had thought he'd reached the point where from now on life would be a series of losses and heartbreaks. Just less and less to live for until one day all that would be left was him and the last star going out. Instead, look at what he had now.

His eyes locked with Donna's, and they were no longer so tired.

'I have never been so happy in my life.'

Let's leave them there, shall we, smiling and happy, friends on a golden day, because up above them, far up above the trees, up and up into the clouds, spinning through the blue sky and into the darkness of space ... off to new adventures ... soars a blue police box.

Move 55

The End

Final Move

Oh, I've not gone. Not just yet.

I'm just making sure all the pieces are where I want them to be. The Doctor, his friends, you.

You're all in a good place.

Exactly where I want you.

Here's the New Doctor, inside his TARDIS, dancing around it as the jukebox plays, flicking switches and pulling levers along to the music, sending the brave little machine off to far shores and distant dreams. And maybe, in a moment, he'll go and put some clothes on.

But for now, he's so happy he's dancing. Because his adventure is only in its opening moves.

This is the beginning.

GAME OVER